NORSE Folktales Myths & Legends

ANIKA HUSSAIN

Illustrated by Kate Forrester

SCHOLASTIC

Published in the UK by Scholastic, 2023
1 London Bridge, London, SE1 9BG
Scholastic Ireland, 89E Lagan Road, Dublin Industrial Estate,
Glasnevin, Dublin, D11 HP5F

ISBN 978-93-5471-731-4

A CIP catalogue record for this book
is available from the British Library.

Printed at Shree Maitrey Printech Pvt. Ltd., Noida

This reprint edition, December 2023

www.scholastic.co.uk

To Tasnim, for all the stories we've shared

CONTENTS

NORWEGIAN FOLKTALES

SWEDISH FOLKTALES

INTRODUCTION

Throughout time, it has been common in Scandinavia for poets and storytellers to share tales that have been passed down orally from generations who were unable to read or write. With their cold, harsh winters and days with limited sunlight, Scandinavians have a long history of brightening the darkness by coming together over stories and shared experiences. Often, people would sit around a blazing fire, warming their hands, as stories kept them alert and awake, children eager to come back the next night for more.

In this collection, we will first explore some favourite tales from Norse mythology. The Norse gods themselves were avid storytellers, believing in the tales the Norns would spin for them, and using them as a blueprint of how to live their lives. Many of the Norse gods' lives were cut short, their fates decided long before they were born, but they made sure that their lives were well-lived and remembered.

The stories of the Norse gods can both inspire and scare you at the same time. You may recognize some of the characters, like Odin, Thor and Loki, as they have appeared in many different guises in books, TV and films over the years.

We will then visit the folktales of Denmark, Norway and Sweden, some of which may also be familiar while others will be brand new to you. The themes of these stories range from bravery and heroism to trickery and magic and often include lessons about gratitude and goodness. You will also stumble upon common things that are found in old traditional stories such as royal weddings, witches and animals that can speak.

What I love most about folktales and myths isn't just the shared experience of them but also how much is left unsaid within them. As these tales were first told many centuries ago, with many years passing before they were written down, there are so many gaps in the stories, allowing me as a reader – or a writer – to try and fill them in myself, pulling me in directions I never could have foreseen. I invite you to do the same as you explore this collection of Norse myths and Scandinavian folktales.

LEGENDS FROM NORSE MYTHOLOGY

Ever since I was a little girl, I've been fascinated by Norse mythology, also known as Scandinavian mythology. Norse mythology is a collection of beliefs and legends that the Nordic people have held dear for centuries, but it wasn't until the thirteenth century that they were written down and made available for the public in the form of Edda, or the plural Eddas: a selection of stories about the Norse gods. These myths would often feature gruesome details and include a lot of death and violence (and were *not* appropriate in school!).

I was particularly fascinated by all the places they are set in. In Norse mythology, there are nine realms or "worlds": Niflheim (the realm of darkness), Muspelheim (the land of fire), Asgard (the realm of the gods), Midgard (the realm of humans), Jotunheim (the realm of giants), Vanaheim (the realm of the Vanir gods, masters of sorcery and magic), Alfheim (the realm of the light elves), Svartalfheim (the realm of dark elves), and Helheim (the realm of the dishonourable dead). By reading about all the different realms, it was as if I had travelled without having to leave my room.

I also really enjoyed getting to know the many prominent figures in Norse mythology. Along with Loki, Thor and Odin, some gods you will encounter are: Frigg (queen of Asgard and Odin's wife), Frey (god of peace and prosperity), Freya (goddess of love), Balder (god of light) and Tyr (god of war), but there are many, many more!

But most of all I was spellbound by Ragnarök, which was the final battle that would end the world; a battle between the gods, led by Odin, and the giants, driven by Loki. There was always a belief that once the apocalyptic event had taken place, with most of the gods dead, two human survivors, Líf and Lífþrasir, would re-emerge from the world tree and populate it once again. There are so many stories in the rich tradition of Norse mythology, and I hope this selection will pique your interest to read more.

HOW THOR LOST HIS HAMMER (AND GOT IT BACK)

In this story, we learn how Thor's legendary hammer, Mjolnir, was stolen from right under his nose and how he managed to retrieve it with some help from the Asgardian gods, the Aesir, and his trickster brother, Loki. This myth is one of the best-known poems from the Poetic Edda*, which is an anonymous collection of Old Norse narrative poems.*

Thor and his hammer, Mjolnir, have always been inseparable. As the only one able to lift it, Thor sees the hammer as an extension of himself. At night, when he sleeps, he keeps Mjolnir close beside him.

Mjolnir is not your typical hammer. When wielded by Thor, it opens interdimensional portals, such as the one to Asgard, and it can summon all the elements – wind, rain, thunder, you name it!

And it is, in fact, the only hammer able to stop the lord of the underworld, Hel.

So it is no surprise that when Thor awoke one morning to find Mjolnir missing, he was distraught.

"LOKI!" Thor bellowed, scrambling around in his bed for the fifth time in case the hammer had been hiding under the sheets all along.

"What?" Loki groaned at having been awoken so early by his brother. "The sun has barely risen. What are you making a ruckus for?"

"Where is Mjolnir?" Thor demanded, not in the mood for his brother's usual antics.

"What do you mean 'where is Mjolnir'?" Loki asked, imitating his brother's deep voice. "He's where he always is!"

"Well, not today he isn't. Somebody must have taken him, and I'm sure it was you, so do yourself a favour and give him to me before I do something I will regret."

Loki furrowed his brows. "But brother, I do not have him!"

Thor looked at his brother, searching for a hint of trickery in his eyes. "Of course you don't have him. You've given him to somebody! In any case, I order you to get him back!"

"No, I swear!" Loki looked just as frazzled as Thor felt at the idea of losing Mjolnir. "I don't have him, and I haven't given him away either."

Thor would have fallen over if Loki hadn't rushed over to hold him up.

"You're telling me … somebody has stolen Mjolnir?" Thor gasped, the hurt in his voice enough to make Loki's bones ache with sympathy.

"It appears so."

Thor couldn't believe it. He had been so certain that Loki had pulled another of his incessant pranks, but now … how would he be able to find Mjolnir? Who could have taken him? Without his hammer, Thor would be putting the entire world and all his fellow gods at risk.

"Though…" Loki began.

"What?"

"I have my suspicions about who might have taken him."

"You do?" Thor's hopes rekindled.

"It must have been those frost giants." Loki shook his head in disgust. "Quick, we need to go find Freya and begin the search for Mjolnir. We can borrow her falcon cloak."

Freya, the goddess of love and fertility, had in her possession a garment made of falcon feathers that could make its wearer look like a bird and grant them the ability to fly.

Thor and Loki swiftly visited Freya in Folkvangar, the Field of Folks. They found her sitting among her maidens and, with an urgency she had never seen before, they explained what grave danger Asgard would be in without her assistance.

"Of course I will lend you my falcon cloak," she said without a second thought.

"I'll go," Loki said to his brother. "You stay here in the event that Mjolnir has simply been misplaced and not been stolen."

Loki dressed himself in the cloak and flew away to the land of the frost giants, Jotunheim, where he hoped to find Mjolnir. After eight days, he arrived. He removed the cloak and transformed back to his usual self before greeting the king of the land, Thrym. Thrym was relaxing in his courtyard, watching as one of his men slowly brushed the mane of one of his horses.

"I have come to fetch Thor's hammer. I have it on good authority that one of your men has taken it," Loki bellowed, hoping Thrym didn't sense his lying.

Thrym merely laughed. "Is that so?"

"Yes! Do not waste my time denying it."

"Well, I will not. But I am no fool. Do you really think I'm going to give it back after all the trouble we have gone through?" The king returned his attention to his horse, ignoring Loki, as if he were a mere mortal and not a god. "No, no. If I were to give Mjolnir back to you, it would only be on one condition."

Loki hesitated, but then asked, "And what is that?"

Thrym sneered as he said, "That Freya be my wife."

Loki guffawed, but the king did not even flinch. "You're serious?"

"Of course I am! She's only the most beautiful goddess in Asgard. I will settle for nothing less."

Loki blinked slowly, as if that would make things clearer for him, but it didn't.

"Well then," said Thrym, "are you going to bring her to me or not?"

Loki could see no way out. He had no choice but to leave the land of the frost giants and break the news to Thor.

He expected Thor to break down in tears at the king's request, but instead all it did was spur Thor into action. Thor, along with his brother, visited the goddess again.

Before Freya could even greet them, Thor yelled, "Put on a wedding dress!"

Freya, startled by the outburst, merely tilted her head to the side in confusion.

"What my brother means," Loki clarified, "is that Thrym will give him Mjolnir back if you agree to marry him."

Freya glanced between the two men before letting out a snort that could have shaken the whole of Asgard. "That is funny, but enough with the jokes."

"It is not a joke," Loki muttered. "Thrym wants you and you only."

"Quick! Mjolnir needs to be retrieved!" Thor nearly grabbed the goddess by the wrist before he caught the murderous look in her eyes and decided against it.

"Mjolnir wouldn't need to be retrieved if you hadn't been so careless in the first place, and I certainly don't think you are in a position to ask me to marry a man in exchange for him." Freya's face lit up with anger. "Now I'd like you to leave before you say something even more foolish than you already have."

Thor and Loki left Freya's home like dogs with tails between their legs. Soon after, they bumped into Odin.

"Thor, Loki – why do you look so downtrodden?" Odin asked, upon seeing their sullen expressions.

They explained everything: how Mjolnir was stolen, Loki's visit to the frost giants and Thrym's demand, before lowering their voices with shame at the proposal they had put forward to Freya.

They'd expected Odin to be just as angry as Freya, but instead his face only scrunched in concern. Perhaps he, like the brothers, couldn't help but worry about what the fate of the gods would be should Thrym choose to trade Mjolnir with somebody else. Somebody with an agenda.

"We must call a meeting of all the Aesir.

Immediately!" Odin's voice boomed. "What's to say that Thrym won't storm Asgard and take Freya to be his wife anyway? No, we cannot do that to her!"

It didn't take any longer than ten minutes – or so it felt, but time moved unusually in Asgard – before the Aesir gathered in the Great Judgement Hall in the Palace of Gladsheim, the biggest and best room built on Earth, made entirely out of gold.

As Odin discussed with his fellow gods the best way to move forward, Heimdall, the watchman of the gods, came up with a solution.

Thor couldn't help but feel embarrassed.

"You want me to what?" he asked, hoping he had misheard.

"You dress up as Freya," Heimdall suggested simply. "Put on a wedding dress, some gems, perhaps even Freya's special necklace, and travel to Jotunheim to get your hammer back." Heimdall turned to Loki. "I'm surprised you haven't suggested this already. Here I thought you were the master of trickery!"

Loki blushed. Heimdall was right. He should have thought of it – it was the perfect deception!

"I will do no such thing!" Thor growled. "You simply want to laugh at my expense. No, I will not do it."

Heimdall shrugged. "If you wanted Mjolnir as badly as you say you do, you would do it in a heartbeat."

"You also don't exactly have the luxury to worry about appearances when the only weapon that can save us in the battle against Ragnarök is with … an enemy," Loki reminded Thor.

Thor wouldn't listen to Loki and Heimdall. He just stomped his feet on the ground like a child refusing to take a bath. But he could not deny that he was desperate for Mjolnir's return, so after his short temper tantrum, he finally said, "Fine, get me the dress."

The Aesir didn't even hesitate before fetching a dress from the goddess that was large enough for Thor. Freya even came along to watch as Thor shimmied into the dress.

"I don't know what I despise more: this plan or you in that dress," she said to Thor.

The dress was too short, the hem landing slightly above Thor's knees, but its skirt, along with its wide sleeves, hid his bulky figure well enough.

Thor looked at himself in the mirror, shaking his head at his outfit. His hair – his gorgeous hair – was covered by a veil, and he could hardly see through the flimsy fabric. He'd thought wearing Freya's necklace, Brisingamen, and bracelets might make him feel better, but it did nothing of the sort. To complete the outfit, he added a pair of rattling keys to his belt.

"Looking good, brother," Loki laughed. But only a second later, the Aesir surrounded him, too, holding garments he had never seen before. "What's this for?"

"You didn't think I'd be the only one going in disguise?" Thor sneered. "After all, a bride needs a lady-in-waiting."

For eight days and nights, through thunder and lightning, the two brothers travelled in Thor's goat-driven chariot all the way to Jotunheim.

Thrym spotted the chariot from afar and nearly wielded his weapon until he saw the dresses flowing in the wind. Freya! The gods had brought her to him!

"Quick, deck the halls! Prepare a welcome party! My wife is coming," he instructed his servants, slicking back the few strands of hair he had left with his own spit. Immediately, Thrym's servants scurried around, chasing goats and rolling barrels of mead to serve at the feast. This was going to be the wedding of the ages after all.

As the chariot touched down in Jotunheim, the bleating of the goats deafening even to Thor, who had grown accustomed to them, the two brothers got ready for the performance of their lives.

"Freya!" Thrym exclaimed. "I am so pleased to see you accepted my offer."

"Of course," Thor said, raising the pitch of his voice in the hope of sounding like the goddess. "And I brought my lady-in-waiting to see me through the festivities."

Loki, no stranger to shapeshifting, had transformed his features to resemble somebody who may as well have been Freya's sister. Of course, Loki could easily have disguised himself as Freya, and looked much more convincing than Thor, but the trickster god had not suggested this idea to his brother. Where would the fun have been in that?

"Come, we have prepared a feast for you, my bride!" The king guided the two brothers into the hall where the wedding was to be held the very next day.

There, they took a seat at the heavily laden banquet table, decorated with giant platters of breads and fruits. To say they were ravenous would be an understatement. Thor in particular, with his huge, strong body, and an enormous appetite, was hungrier than ever after their long journey. Thrym had barely sat down before Thor scarfed a whole ox, eight salmon, three kegs of mead and an entire wedding cake.

"Oh my," Thrym said, his voice filled with awe. "Never have I see somebody eat or drink so much."

Loki shot daggers at his brother with his eyes. If Thor continued eating at that pace, the frost giant would see through their disguises in no time.

"My king," Loki said, feigning embarrassment, "do forgive us. Freya hasn't eaten in eight days. She was so desperate and excited to be wed to you that she would not even stop for a meal on our journey. That's why she's so hungry now."

Thor looked up from stuffing his face, his eyes widening as he realized his mistake, before beaming at his brother with pride. He always knew Loki was a good liar, but even Thor almost fell for that one!

Unfortunately for him, Loki's lie only made Thrym more eager to kiss his bride. "Come here, my beautiful goddess!" he cried.

Before Thor had a chance to fend off the king, Thrym had lifted his veil and was met with Thor's fiery red eyes.

"Argh!" the king recoiled in fear. "What is wrong with my Freya's eyes?"

"Oh," Loki responded with a grave tone. "You see, Freya hasn't slept in eight days. Again, she was simply too excited to marry you that she couldn't rest!"

Satisfied again, Thrym stared at "Freya" with adoration. He was so infatuated that he could not see past the deception.

A little while later, Thrym's sister barged into the dining hall and demanded the dowry that Freya was to pay on behalf of her family.

"It is an honour to marry my brother, and you must pay the price," she ordered.

Thor and Loki exchanged glances. Wordlessly they gave away a few of the rings they had "borrowed" from Freya as payment. They figured it wasn't like she'd notice anyway – she got new jewellery all the time.

As the night passed, Thrym grew more and more besotted by his bride. Even when she did not speak, his eyes brimmed with adoration.

At last he exclaimed, "I cannot wait a minute longer. Freya will be my bride tonight! We must proceed with the blessing of Var!" Turning to his servants, he ordered them to bring Thor's hammer.

They came back, after what felt like for ever, with Mjolnir in hand. Thor had to stop himself from leaping up and grabbing it from them. As was customary, the hammer was brought and laid across the bride's knees as a form of blessing in the name of Var, the goddess of wedding vows.

As the hammer came to rest in front of him, Thor's heart did somersaults. He could barely contain himself. Before he knew what he was doing, he'd picked it up, removed his veil and ripped off his dress to reveal his armour, showing himself not to be Freya at all.

"Where is my bride?!" Thrym screamed with disgust. "What have you done to her?"

"Oh, Thrym, do you not know better than to steal from a god?" Thor cried. "Now unless you want me to devour you, your sister and all your servants, we shall be leaving with Mjolnir."

Thrym was shocked and ashamed that he had been so easily fooled, but with the powerful hammer clasped in Thor's mighty hands, he saw no other option than to admit defeat. With great resignation, he let the god and his smug "lady-in-waiting" return to their goat-driven chariot and fly back to Asgard with their prize.

And that is the tale of how Thor lost his hammer to the king of the frost giants – and, with a little trickery, got it back.

HOW FRIGG OUTSMARTED ODIN

This particular tale from Norse mythology shows us that even a powerful and revered god like Odin can fall prey to trickery! This legend was first told in the seventh-century Origo Gentis Langobardorum *and then in the eighth century by Oskar the Deacon in his* Historia Langobardorum. *The Langobards, which are descendants of Germanic people, ruled a region that is now known as Italy.*

Odin was bored.

Despite being the All-Father, the god who rules over all others, he often found that his life was quite normal. In many ways, it was uncomplicated (at least for a king!) and, surprisingly, humdrum. Now you must be wondering how the life of a *god*, especially one of *war*, could be so boring?

It's simple: it gets dull when you're not in on the action. Yes, Odin had certainly been on many great adventures, but things had changed over his lifetime. These days, he played a major role when it came to handing out advice and gifts to warriors preparing for the battles of their lives, but while they partook in the war, Odin did not. Rather, he acted as a referee.

After carefully analysing battles, Odin would decide which side would come out victorious. He also decided whether the slain would find a home in Valhalla – warrior paradise – or if they were to end up in more despicable places – like the cold and dark Helheim.

It wasn't easy being Odin, as being a god never is, but making decisions all on your own can get tiresome after a while. And he wasn't quiet about this predicament either.

"What?" his wife, Frigg, asked after he had sighed for the thousandth time that morning.

"I am *bored*!" Odin complained. "There is nothing to do these days except spectate from afar. I want *excitement*." Odin sulked like a child, his chin resting on his fist.

Frigg simply shook her head. "Be careful what you wish for, my dear husband. You never know what may happen..."

Odin should have listened to his wife.

It all started when conflict broke out between two Germanic tribes, the Vandals and the Winnilers. As the two tribes prepared for battle, the leaders of each side asked Odin to declare them victorious, begging for the war to be over quickly. Every day for a week, they would visit Odin to make their case, highlighting their strengths and values to secure his bet.

But Odin took his time in making his decision. Despite sitting on Hlidskjalf, his throne in Asgard from which he observed the Nine Worlds, he could not see clearly. Boredom clouded his judgement and motivation. It was taking him so long to decide that Frigg had to intervene.

"Odin, please could you hurry up and grant the Winnilers victory?"

She sat on the throne next to her husband's, where they both watched over the entire universe. Their thrones sat in Odin's hall, Valaskjálf, which was larger than any castle you could ever imagine and roofed with pure silver.

"And why should the Winnilers be victorious, my queen?" Odin asked as he took a swig of his mead.

"The Vandals can hardly keep themselves upright! You've seen them at battle practice. The Winnilers have grace and agility. It is clear as day that they could beat the Vandals!"

Odin let out a scoff. "The Winnilers are made up of women. They would not stand a chance before the Vandals."

"Odin, my love, you cannot disregard the Winnilers simply because they are women!"

Odin could sense that he was playing with fire. "Of course not, my queen. Women are extraordinary beings – just look at you."

Frigg ignored the god's attempt at flattery. "What will it take for you to see that I am right?"

Odin thought about it.

"My dearest Frigg, how about this? Instead of arguing back and forth, why don't we simply award victory to the tribe I see first in the morning?"

Frigg's expression tightened as she considered her husband's suggestion. She realized what he was doing: he was attempting to trick her. Frigg knew as well as Odin that the Vandals would be the only tribe visible through the window next to Odin's side of the bed the next morning, as they would approach Valaskjálf from the east while the Winnilers would approach from the west to enter into battle. Odin's window faced the east, so the Vandals would be granted automatic victory. Odin was trying to outsmart his queen, but he underestimated her, just as he dismissed the Winnilers for being a tribe of women.

Odin, more than anybody, should have known not to even attempt to trick Frigg. Frigg had already outsmarted him once before, but she knew that the topic of Geirröth and Agnar was still a sore spot for him. If she brought up the past, she would be forced to deal with a whiny god. Instead, Frigg played along. She had no problem outwitting her husband once again.

"Why don't we bet on it?" Frigg asked with a sly smirk.

Odin, never one to turn away from a wager, especially one he was certain he would win, couldn't resist the bait. "What do you have in mind?"

"Bragging rights. What else?"

Odin shook his head with a laugh. "Then bragging rights it is. But my dear Frigg, don't say I didn't warn you!"

As Odin and Frigg prepared for bed that night, Frigg couldn't help but feel her entire being reeling with energy. She couldn't wait to see Odin's face when he realized just how wrong he was – about both the Winnilers and his queen. The two gods got into bed, and within only a few moments the room filled with the sound of snoring.

Odin had fallen asleep. But Frigg? Frigg was very much awake. She crept out of bed, careful not to make a sound as she sneaked out of their abode to go and speak with the leader of the Winniler tribe.

"My dear queen, to what do I owe this pleasure?" the leader of the tribe asked, looking absolutely petrified to have been visited by the goddess herself at such an ungodly hour.

"I'm here to help you," Frigg said simply. "I would like to ensure you are victorious in the battle against the Vandals."

The leader gasped. "How, my queen?"

"Before you approach our great dwelling tomorrow, you must..." Frigg lowered her voice, afraid Odin might have awoken and sent spies her way. "… reposition your hair."

"Come again? Did you say 'hair'?" the leader asked, sure she must have misheard the goddess.

Frigg nodded. "I need you and your warriors to reposition your hair so that it appears you have long beards."

"But why, my queen?"

"My husband seems to think that women cannot be victorious, and I am going to prove him wrong. All we need is a little deception. Now hurry, gather your tribe and find a way to tie those manes into beards by morning. I must go now!"

Frigg hurried back to her home and found her husband still in a deep sleep. This was fortunate, because Frigg's plan was not yet complete.

While asking the Winniler women to tie their hair into beards was one part of the scheme, the second required a rearrangement of the room. You see, on Frigg's side of the bed, there was an identical window facing west. If she could ensure Odin looked that way in the morning, he would see the Winniler tribe instead of the Vandals.

As Odin snored on, Frigg used all her strength to rotate the bed, so that Odin faced Frigg's window.

Frigg was so nervous – no, *excited* – to see her husband's reaction that as soon as the first light of dawn arrived, she plugged his nose and startled him awake. Odin bolted upright, trying to regain his breath, before rubbing the sleep out of his eyes and looking to the left, as he usually would, to see out of the window.

In the early morning light, just as Odin had predicted, he saw a passing tribe of bearded men on their way to the battlefield. He grinned to himself as he turned to his wife.

"There we have it! As I promised, these warriors will be the rightful victors."

Frigg hoped Odin could not read the anticipation in her face as she peered casually in his direction. "Of course, my king, as we agreed. Victory will be awarded to the Winniler tribe."

"The *Winniler* tribe?" Odin was suddenly wide awake. He bolted out of bed to peer out of the window. Surely that couldn't be – Frigg must have been mistaken. Odin had been certain the Vandals would appear on his side of the bed … and these warriors were men, were they not? They had long beards!

Then, looking around the room in disorientation,

Odin realized that the layout had changed. The window he had been looking out of was not the window on *his* side.

It was on *Frigg's* side.

Not only that, but as the group of warriors neared, he noticed that they were women indeed, with their long hair tied around their faces. Odin turned to see a wide, devious grin on his queen's face, her sharp teeth gleaming. At that moment, Odin could not even be hurt or angered by her tricks, but rather impressed by the lengths his clever wife would go to outsmart him.

Frigg got out of bed and joined Odin by the window. "A promise is a promise," she said, caressing his rough cheek.

"And so it is," Odin said, now more in love with his queen than he had ever been. "The Winnilers are to be granted victory."

And that is the story of how Frigg outsmarted Odin, reminding him that even someone as mighty and powerful as the All-Father could be outplayed, that women should never be underestimated – and that if he ever complained of boredom again, she would be sure to keep him on his toes!

THE BINDING OF FENRIR

In this tale, Odin decides he must control the wolf, Fenrir, a child of Loki. But binding a wolf, particularly a child of the trickster god, is not simple… While the story focuses on Jörmungand, Hel and Fenrir, Loki had many other children – but it was thought that Jörmungand, Hel and Fenrir posed the biggest threat to Asgard as a whole and are therefore the most prominent in Norse mythology. Loki's other children include Sleipnir, Odin's eight-legged horse, and Narvi and Vali, who Loki had with his wife, Sigyn.

One day, Odin sat on his throne, overlooking all the worlds. He was expecting nothing out of the ordinary, when suddenly his stomach turned with anxiety.

"What's wrong?" Frigg asked him. She leaned closer to see what her husband was looking at and realized why the All-Father had suddenly gone so quiet. "Oh."

Before Odin's eyes, he could see three children of the mischievous Loki – Jörmungand, Hel and Fenrir – each offspring taunting the people of Asgard. Until now, their existence had not troubled Odin, but he could not ignore them any longer: they were growing up fast, and the strength he was sure they possessed from their wicked father could be a threat to his sacred Asgard.

"What will you do?" Frigg asked her husband.

Odin was torn. The children were teenagers after all, and they shouldn't be punished for the sins of their father. But what else could he do? He had to protect Asgard, and seeing them taunting his people made him think they had inherited a heinous side not only from their father but also their mother, Angrboda, the mother of all monsters.

Odin discussed with the other gods what to do

about the children and the answer was clear: they must be captured.

"Their mother is evil!"

"And so is their father!"

"How can anything good come from such horrendous beings?"

And so the gods agreed that Loki's children had to be kidnapped and taken to Asgard, where Odin would decide what to do with them next.

It did not take long for a group of gods to cross into Jotunheim by night. There they stormed into Angrboda's home and bound her to her throne as she watched her children being carried out and away to Asgard.

When Odin set his eyes on the three children, he knew what to do immediately.

He sent Jörmungand, the serpent, down into the deepest depths of the ocean, where he was to live for the rest of his life coiled around Midgard. Jörmungand later became known as the "Midgard Serpent" and became so long that he could encircle the whole Earth with his body and take his tail in his mouth. When Jörmungand tried to rise from the bottom of the ocean, waves would dash high and powerful storms would capsize even the strongest of ships.

When Odin set his eyes on the serpent's sister, Hel, a female being, he threw her out of Asgard, too, but rather than send her to the bottom of the ocean with her brother, she was sent to Niflheim, the world beneath the worlds that was shrouded in darkness. In Niflheim, Hel was sentenced to look after the most wicked people who had died.

And then, finally, Odin laid his eyes on the youngest child: a wolf, Fenrir. While the wolf looked strong, he did not seem to possess the same evil as his siblings.

"Why don't we keep him in Asgard?" one of the gods suggested to Odin. "Perhaps the evil is not within him, and even if a little of it lurks, we could tame it?"

"What do you mean?" Odin asked.

"By living with the Aesir and seeing all the good in our world, he might become docile. I mean, he looks no different than any other wolf. The other two..." The god shook his head. "They looked like trouble. This one seems fine."

Odin agreed. He could see no harm in allowing the wolf to be kept as a pet in Asgard.

Except, of course, there would be.

Day by day, the wolf became bigger, stronger

and fiercer. His growl was loud, and he could bite the hand off any god. Soon enough, there was only one person brave enough to dare feed him – Tyr, son of Odin and god of war and justice.

As each day passed, Fenrir became larger, his bite more vicious.

"We need to do something about him," the gods said to Odin. "He's becoming more dangerous by the day."

"And," the three Norns said in unison, "we have reason to believe that the wolf will be the death of you, All-Father."

That anxiety Odin felt at the beginning of this story? It was back. And it was stronger than before. Because the Norns were the deities responsible for shaping the gods' fates.

"It's decided then," said the gods. "Something needs to be done."

"But what? It's not like he can be killed. He is our kin and we do not kill family, even if he is descended from the treacherous Loki. We cannot shed blood within the realms of Asgard."

The gods debated what to do. They had to guard their home, and their people, against Fenrir but their options were limited.

"We shall bind him," said Odin at last. "We will make a chain mightier than any other with the help of Thor's hammer, Mjolnir, and with it Fenrir shall be bound once and for all!"

They soon got to work. Odin immediately sought out Thor and explained what was needed of him.

"For you, I will work all night long," Thor declared and he stuck to his word: all night the people of Asgard could hear Mjolnir forging a chain strong enough to hold back the wolf.

The next evening, Thor brought the newly made chain to the gods at the meeting place, Odin's palace of Gladsheim.

"Now let's try it!" they said.

Idun, Kvasir and some of the other gods brought in Fenrir, who came willingly. He thought nothing of the gods standing together awaiting him. In fact, he allowed himself to be bound by the chain, letting Thor wrap it around his neck and legs.

Thor felt proud as he fastened together the final links, and the gods were just praising him for his excellent work when Fenrir took a single step forward. Barely flexing a muscle, Fenrir's massive paws broke the chain as if it were nothing but yarn.

"That ... wasn't meant to happen," Thor mumbled

as the gods sprang back with alarm. "But fear not, I will make another chain. A much stronger chain!"

Thor could not bear watching his work be torn into pieces again, so he worked for three nights and three days to forge a chain strong enough to restrain the wolf. As Thor worked, many others came and watched the hammer fall upon the metal with quick blows. Some even sang to Thor to cheer him on.

While all of this happened, Fenrir himself sneaked peeks at Thor's handiwork, before walking away with a quiet, confident laugh.

When the three nights had passed, the chain was finally finished. This one was heavier than the first, and Thor had to drag it into the palace, unable to lift it.

When Fenrir caught sight of the chain, his confidence was not quite so high as it had been when he watched Thor work. This time, he was not so willing to be bound and instead the gods had to trick him.

"Are you scared?" Ullr, the god of winter and hunting, teased.

"Not at all!" Fenrir responded, though it was a lie.

"It's only a chain. You so easily tore the other one, are you worried you won't manage with this one?"

Fenrir hesitated.

"If you break this chain, which we're sure you can, you'll be known throughout all Nine Worlds for your strength, Fenrir. And who wouldn't want that?" asked Ullr.

Fenrir couldn't disagree and allowed the gods to wind the chain around his neck and legs.

As Thor watched the other gods struggle to wrap the chain around the wolf, he was certain that this was the one. He had faith in Mjolnir that the wolf would not escape this time.

Though that faith did not last long – as with one great shake, Fenrir managed to break free of the chain once again. There was a horrible clanging of metal as the chain clattered to the ground. To make matters worse, Fenrir smashed his huge paw down on to one of the links, causing it to shatter into pieces and shoot in every direction like shrapnel.

"I shall never be bound! Any chain you make for me, I shall break!" he snarled, before heading to his lair on the other side of the bridge, just beyond the Glacier Peaks.

Thor, Odin and the other gods stood in silence,

unable to comprehend what had happened or what to do next.

A few hours later, they reconvened.

"We need to visit the elves," said Frey, the god of summer. "I might not be as brave as Tyr or have battled like Thor, but I have seen a lot in the forests, and what I have noticed is how the greatest power can lie in the unexpected. I have seen how the elves are able to make great and powerful weapons out of next to nothing. If there's anyone who can save us, it is them!"

Odin's troubled expression remained but he knew his options were slim. "Send a messenger to Svartalfheim," he commanded, "and have them make a chain as soon as possible."

Frey travelled far inside the Earth, under Midgard, until they reached Svartalfheim, where the elves were hard at work in the warm and wet forest. Inside a gloomy and twilit grotto they found the king of the elves.

"Odin requires a chain," Frey said without any pleasantries, "and we require your workers to make it. In exchange, he will give you as much gold as you could possibly want."

The king's eyes glittered with the idea of gold,

even if it did come from Odin. They had never been big fans of his, but they dared not disobey him either. After all, he was the reason they had to work underground.

"It will take two days and nights to make the chain," the king said.

"That sounds reasonable," Frey replied, but in the back of his mind he worried. It had taken Thor three days and nights to make his chain and it hadn't been successful, so how could the elves succeed in less time?

"It will be stronger than any of you have seen before, trust me," the king said, as if he could read Frey's mind.

The king set his men to work, and Frey was astounded, as he always was, by the way the elves retrieved coal and diamonds from the fire that burned in the centre of the Earth. He watched as they banged and folded various types of metals, stringing them together to form armour, weapons and anything else they wanted. He felt reassured by their deft hard work and skill. Soon they would make a powerful chain.

After two days, the dark elf king visited Frey, holding out a small and fine chain to him.

"It may be small and look weak," he said, "but trust me when I say it is made of the six strongest things we could find."

"And they are?"

"The sound of a cat moving, the beards of women, the roots of mountains, the spittle of birds, the voice of fish and the sinews of a bear," replied the king.

Frey was sceptical. These things did not sound especially strong! "And … you're sure this will hold Fenrir?"

The king nodded. "Have you ever wondered why a cat seems to make no noise when it moves or why women's beards are never seen? Ah, for they are with the elves for safekeeping! They are simply too mighty for you to behold them. Trust me, Frey, this chain can never be broken, and once it is placed on Fenrir it will never be taken off again. Take my word for it."

And Frey did. He presented the chain to the gods, telling them about the six ingredients that had gone into the delicate chain. While sceptical, they, too, came around to trust the king's word. The elves were masterful craftsmen and to doubt them would be to doubt their whole existence.

Again, they approached Fenrir and coaxed him to be bound. This time, however, they invited him to go out with them to the island of Lyngvi, which looked like the crater of an extinct volcano, and hoped to tie him to a giant rock. When the gods showed Fenrir the chain, the wolf laughed.

"What are you laughing at? It's stronger than it seems!" said one of the gods.

"Of course it is," Fenrir snorted.

"You won't be able to break it, that's for sure," taunted Frey.

"It's so delicate anybody could. It's an insult to even try to bind me with it." Fenrir was confident in his strength, until he thought further. "Unless … magic has gone into making this chain. In which case, you can keep it to yourself. I won't have it wound around my legs!"

"We thought you could break through any chain we made for you. Are you telling us you've been lying…"

Fenrir was not having been called a liar.

"No, I can break through any chain you make for me," he growled, his teeth gleaming in the low light. "Though I will not stand for trickery. As such, I will only be bound if one of you put your hand in my mouth as a token that you are not deceiving me with a chain bound by magic."

The gods looked at one another without a word and slowly stepped back, not willing to put their limbs at risk, until only one brave person remained standing: Tyr. He knew magic had gone into the chain, but he also knew there was no other way to restrain Fenrir.

"As you wish," Tyr told Fenrir as he lifted his right arm and put his hand in the wolf's mouth. As he did so, the gods got to work and wound Fenrir's neck and legs with the delicate chain, fastening it around a rock.

When they were done, Fenrir began to struggle, kicking and shaking, but the more he moved the tighter the rope wound around him.

"No, this cannot be!" he snarled. "You tricked me, and for this you shall pay!"

And Fenrir clamped his jaws down on Tyr's hand. Tyr twisted in pain, crying out for all Nine Worlds to hear.

But Tyr did not let his pain overshadow the victory for long: Tyr had dared risk his right hand for the peace and happiness of Asgard, and Fenrir was successfully bound.

Content with the outcome, the gods returned to Asgard, rejoicing in their triumph.

Even so, Odin could not shake his brewing anxiety. They may have bound Fenrir, but the three Norns had still prophesied that the wolf would be the death of him.

He could not help but wonder: would it still come true…?

THE DEATH OF BALDER

This story recounts how Frigg and Odin's son, Balder, was murdered by his own brother due to Loki's deception, even when Frigg had gone to incredible lengths to ensure Balder's invulnerability.

Balder, the god of light, was suffering from nightmares.

Specifically, nightmares about his own death.

But Balder did not want to tell anybody about his dreams, especially his mother and father, Frigg and Odin, because he did not want to burden them. So he kept his sorrows and worries to himself.

It did not take long however before the two gods saw the light in their son's eyes disappear.

"Whatever is going on with Balder?" Frigg asked Odin one day. "He is no longer himself. Have you noticed?"

Odin nodded. "Yes, something is different about him. But perhaps it is just a phase he is going through. Growing pains, as they say."

Frigg tried not to worry about her son but couldn't help herself. This was her child after all. So one night, Frigg finally asked Balder what it was that made his head hang with weariness.

"I've been having dreams," Balder confessed.

"About what?" Frigg asked.

Balder hesitated. "Dreams of darkness. About my death."

Frigg gasped before throwing her arms around her son. She could hardly believe what he was saying. When gods dreamed, it was usually prophetic ... and this was one prophecy she did not want to come true.

It didn't take long before Frigg shared her son's worries with her husband.

"We must do something, Odin," she said. "We cannot allow these dreams to continue. We must make him secure against all that can endanger him."

And Frigg wasted no time in doing just that. Desperate for a chance to save her son, Frigg gathered her servants and sent them throughout the Nine Worlds with the strictest of instructions: "I want all entities, living or non-living, be that animals, fish, stones or trees, to swear an oath that they will never harm my Balder. All creations must swear by this oath. Understood?"

Her servants spurred into action and did as their queen asked of them. When they returned, they said that all creation but one had sworn the oath.

"Who dare not swear the oath?" Frigg demanded.

"Mistletoe," said one servant. "But there is no need to fear mistletoe, my queen, for we cannot see how it could ever harm Balder."

Frigg agreed with the servants and left it at that,

pleased by the idea that almost all entities – even the strongest ones such as torrential rain and the most venomous of animals – had sworn the oath.

But Odin was not as reassured as his wife. Even after the sworn oaths, he still feared what might happen to his son. With this in mind, he saddled his eight-legged horse, Sleipnir, and rode to the underworld to seek Hel as she could tell who was to arrive next in her realm of the dead.

"You have rudely awoken me. What for?" she asked as she rubbed the sleep out of her eyes.

"For my son, Balder, the god of light." Odin looked around the dark room, which seemed to have been prepared for whoever was to pass next. "For whom is this room being made up?"

"Well, it is for him – your own son, Balder."

Odin's breath caught in his throat. "Who is it that will slay him? I must know now."

"His own brother, Hodur, will slay him," Hel said, getting ready to sink back into her sleep. "But I also know this: you will bear a son to avenge his death."

Odin could not believe Hel. Why would Hodur, Balder's twin brother, slay him? Odin returned to Asgard and told his wife what he had found out.

Frigg however was not worried.

"Nothing can hurt Balder, Odin. I've made sure of it. All entities, living and non-living, have sworn the oath." Frigg caressed her husband's grey beard. "Now come, rejoice with me, for this horn of mead is as delicious and fresh as nothing I have ever tasted before."

Odin did as his wife instructed but could not help the ever-expanding pit in his stomach.

Even so, life in Asgard continued and, in fact, lots of fun was being had. The gods had invented a new game that kept them entertained for days. At mealtimes in Valhalla, the majestic hall within Asgard, it only seemed appropriate that the gods hurl things at Balder and see what happened. They were all so amused by the way the items looped, spiralled and bounced off the god of light without any ramifications whatsoever. No matter how hard the gods threw, the objects would rarely even touch Balder, and even though they knew this, they kept trying even harder to see if anything would stick.

The only one who was not having fun? Loki. He didn't understand why everybody was so pleased with themselves about the god's invulnerability. Also, he didn't like all the attention he was receiving.

Loki should have been the talk of the party, not Odin's measly son, Balder!

He disguised himself as an elderly woman and went to Fensalir, the home of Frigg, where Frigg was spinning her wheel while she took a break from all the festivities taking place in Valhalla.

"What is going on there?" Loki asked, pointing at the gods throwing items at Balder. One good thing about Fensalir was the ability to overlook Gladsheim!

Frigg did not bat an eyelid at the woman who she had never seen before. Perhaps she was simply a newcomer to Asgard. "Oh, they think it's such fun to throw things at my son to test out his invulnerability!"

"Invulnerability you say?"

"Oh yes, nothing can harm my dear Balder! All entities swore an oath." Frigg smiled to herself before frowning. "Well, nearly all entities. There is one that did not. Though I don't worry much about it. It's merely mistletoe, and it is far too small and soft to do harm anyway."

"Ah, what a lucky man your boy is," Loki commented before exiting to see Balder's invulnerability in action in Valhalla.

Loki quickly headed outside to the gates where he

knew a sycamore growing mistletoe. There, with a wicked smile on his lips and treachery in his heart, he picked some of the mistletoe – before casting a spell that strengthened and moulded it into an arrow.

Loki inspected his new weapon before heading back inside to where the gods stood around Balder, still throwing things at him and laughing. The only one who stood apart from the crowd was Balder's twin brother, Hodur, the god of darkness.

"Why don't you join your fellow gods in testing your brother's invulnerability?" Loki asked Hodur in a low voice.

Hodur sighed. "Well, I cannot see anything and therefore cannot take aim." Hodur had lost his sight in battle many years before. "Besides, I have no weapon to throw at him."

The devious Loki couldn't help himself. It was almost as if the pieces had fallen into place.

"What if I were to be your eyes?" he offered. "And I have a weapon right here in my hands that you could throw."

Loki placed the arrow in Hodur's hand.

"This seems awfully light. What is it made of?" Hodur asked.

"Nothing to concern your mind with. Now let it fly..."

Loki drew back Hodur's hand before letting it go – and then the arrow whizzed through the air and hit the brightly smiling Balder in the chest. Balder managed only to look down at the arrow piercing him before falling to his death.

Where there was usually laughter at how Balder could avoid anything thrown at him, there was now only a deafening silence. For some time, all gods stood motionless, horrified, wondering who in Asgard could have known the one thing that could have killed Balder and dared to throw it. Amidst their shock, Loki slipped silently away.

"My son!" Frigg burst into tears at the sight of her fallen child. "Who dared do this to him?"

"Mother, I think it must have been my arrow," Hodur said, crestfallen. "But it was Loki who gave me the arrow and who drew my arm back to aim it. Loki is behind this!"

The gods murmured among themselves. If it hadn't been for their rule of not killing within Asgard, they would have murdered Hodur for his betrayal that instant.

Frigg shook her head in disbelief. She had done

so much to secure her son's life and yet it had been taken. There was only one thing left to do.

"Who among the gods will win my love and goodwill and offer Hel a reward if she lets Balder come home to Asgard? I'm sure there must be somebody here!" Frigg was distraught and she could not think of anything else. "We cannot live happily without him. He is the god of light after all!"

"I will, my queen," said Hermod, another of her and Odin's sons.

"Then go forth, my son. And quickly!"

Right away, Hermod jumped on Sleipnir and travelled to Niflheim to see Hel. There, he struck a deal with her.

"He can return only on one condition," she said.

"And what's that?" asked Hermod.

"Every living creature and every object on this earth must weep for Balder," she said.

When Hermod returned to Asgard after nine days and nine nights, he told the gods of Hel's answer, and they swiftly sent out messengers all over the world to weep for Balder. Soon enough, all things wept for him: beasts, birds, metals, stones. All over the world, teardrops were shed in the millions, until they met an old woman alone in a cave who, when they asked her to shed a tear for Balder, refused.

"Why should I care?" the woman asked. "Balder is no use to me, alive or dead. Let Hel keep him!"

"Please, you must," one of the messengers pleaded. "It is for the good of Asgard. With Balder's death ... it will be the beginning of Ragnarök."

The old woman merely shrugged. "Then so be it."

As the messengers turned to return to Asgard, one of them caught a glimpse of the old woman's true face: Loki. Loki, in the midst of his joy at killing Balder, had accidentally shown his true form.

When they returned to Asgard, they hung their heads in shame in front of Frigg.

"I'm sorry, my queen. One woman alone would not weep for Balder."

Frigg fell on to her hands and knees, shedding tears for the son she would never see again. In this moment, she vowed to punish Loki for his role in the death of Balder.

She just had to figure out how.

THE PUNISHMENT OF LOKI

After causing the death of Balder, the treacherous Loki is hunted down by the gods of Asgard to pay for the damage he has caused, once and for all… Although Loki had been punished by the gods many times before – when he stole Freya's necklace or cut off the hair of Thor's wife, Sif – now he would learn that he could no longer get away with his antics.

To say that Loki was enemy number one would be an understatement.

For so many years, the gods had allowed him to roam around without consequences, playing his tricks on the entities of Asgard without a care, living up to his name as the god of mischief. But this time the gods would not let him get away with his behaviour, not after his part in the death of Balder.

After deceiving Hodur to fling the arrow of mistletoe at Balder's chest, Loki had swiftly left, knowing that he could never return to Asgard again. Perhaps Loki had gone too far this time. He hadn't realized that the gods would actually punish him. They hadn't before. But, to be fair, this time he had slain the god of light, quite literally clouding Asgard in darkness.

Loki hid deep in the mountains by Franang's Falls, where he hoped nobody would ever find him. He built a hut with doors overlooking each direction so that if someone came for him, he could see them approaching and escape through the opposite door.

He spent his days quite peacefully in the mountains, but as one would expect from the god of mischief, he quickly got bored. Loki wanted excitement and, unfortunately, being by oneself away from anybody else was far from it.

"I need to stay away from the gods, but I want to be near them at the same time. How can I do that?" Loki asked himself. He looked down at the stream by his hut and the little fish that were swimming there. "Perhaps if I turned myself into a fish, they wouldn't be able to catch me! I'd be far too slippery for their callous hands and no hook would be quick enough to sink into me. Though there are nets, and Rán, the goddess of the sea, has one that can capture any sea-goers and I'd rather not be caught in that!"

Loki kept thinking about Rán and her net. How was it made in the first place? It seemed able to capture anything – Idun's apples, grocery carts, an assortment of floe – but surely some entities would be able to escape it? The more Loki thought about it, the more he wished he could make his own net and figure out how to avoid getting caught. If he did that, then he could finally leave this miserable hut and be near enough to the gods again to cause mischief without getting captured.

For nearly four days, Loki sat by a raging fire

in his hut and used a cord he had found in the mountains to make a net. He was nearly finished with the net when he looked up to see two gods in the distance coming towards him from the east.

"Oh no, they've come to capture me!"

Loki quickly threw the net into the fire, not wanting to leave behind any evidence, then ran through one of his doors to the stream, where he leaped in as a salmon. Loki swam along the stream faster than he ever had before, convinced that he would be safe for another day.

But Loki shouldn't have been so confident. When the gods entered his hut, they immediately noticed the burning fish net in the fire.

"No living creature in the Nine Worlds ever escapes Odin's eyes, does it?" said Kvasir, one of the wisest gods in Asgard, after picking out the net. "And sure enough Loki's been here. Look, he must have made this net. He always was good at fishing."

"We were not fast enough," Njord, the god of the wind and sea, said. "He's not here any more. Where could he be?"

"Perhaps he's turned himself into a fish?" Sif, the goddess of harvest, proposed. "He does love a disguise."

"You're right. He's probably been making a net just to figure out how to get out of one!" said Kvasir.

With the new revelation of where Loki could be hiding, the gods spent the rest of the night making a net based on the one they rescued from the fire, and at dawn they headed to the bank of the stream where they hoped to find Loki.

Thor arrived to help them, and together the gods began to drag the net through the river, the salmon swimming downstream in front of them. The first time they did this, Loki managed to hide between two rocks and, even luckier for him, the net was so light that it stayed close to the surface and barely grazed him.

"You'll never catch me!" Loki grinned to himself. He knew that they wouldn't be able to hear him through the deafening splashes of the water, but even so he loved to tease.

When the gods brought up their net, Thor couldn't help but curse. "Why aren't we catching him? Or anything for that matter?" he asked.

Kvasir inspected the net. "It's too light. The fish are simply swimming under it rather than through it. We need to weigh it down."

The three gods grabbed a large boulder from the

nearby bank and tied it to the end of the net. This time, as they once again dragged the net through the river, Loki saw no way of avoiding capture unless he leaped over the net. With no other choice, Loki charged ahead and sprang into the air.

Unluckily for him, Thor was quicker than he had expected!

Quickly Thor waded out into the stream and once again threw the net. Although Loki managed to evade the net, he did not manage to escape Thor's clutch. Despite his slithering, Thor grabbed him and held on tight, Thor's fingers pinching the slippery salmon by its tail.

"Gotcha!" Thor said to Loki before he and the other gods took him into a twilit cave. There was no way they would spill Loki's blood in Gladsheim, one of the many realms of Asgard, but here on the ground of Midgard? It was all fair game.

"What will you do to me?" Loki asked once he had transformed back to his old self. He was shivering, his clothes wet from his excursion as a fish.

"How about a family reunion?" Thor wore a wicked grin that scared Loki and revealed that, before joining the other gods, he had been busy capturing Loki's wife, Sigyn, and their two sons,

Vali and Narvi. He had them brought out in front of Loki now.

"What … what are you going to do to them?" Loki's voice quivered.

"Since you've shown us your true nature by killing Balder, don't you think it's only fair that your sons also show theirs?"

"No, you wouldn't… If you do…"

"Oh, don't worry," said Thor. "We won't turn both of them into their true forms. Only one of them."

Before Loki could ask why, Thor used his magic to reveal Vali's true form. In front of their eyes, Vali transformed into a wolf, his sharp teeth gleaming. Only a second later, overcome by his predator instincts, he leaped on to his brother, Narvi, and sunk his teeth into him.

"No!" Loki cried as he watched the attack on his son.

When Vali had finished, he realized what he had done. He howled in sorrow before running away from the cave, disappearing once and for all. Tears pooled in Loki's eyes like oceans. He couldn't believe what he had just witnessed.

"And now," Thor said, retrieving the rope they

had used to make the nets, "we will bind you to this rock."

Loki was then pinned to a large rock, as his hands and feet were tied to it with the rope. Then Thor called in the giantess of frost, Skadi, who had been waiting outside for just this moment. She fastened a snake to a stalactite high above Loki's head so that it dangled above him.

"What's this for? Is my son's death not enough?" Loki cried.

"For what you did to Balder, never," Thor said through gritted teeth. "You shall suffer for all that you have done."

"The snake will drip venom on to your face as your eternal punishment. Here, let's test it out," said the giantess. She pinched the snake and its venom dropped right on to Loki's cheek, causing him to howl in pain.

"You helped the gods kill my father," Skadi sneered. "You deserve all that is coming your way and more!"

Loki knew he had angered so many, but he was horrified to be left like this. "You can't just abandon me here!" he yelled, straining against his binds.

"Watch us," Thor said, before he, the other gods and Skadi left the cave.

Loki was then left in the cave to suffer his gruesome consequences. Sometimes he was visited by his wife, Sigyn, who would hold a wooden bowl above his head to collect the venom. But when the bowl was filled to the brim, she would have to go to the rock basin miles away to discard the fermenting pool of poison, leaving Loki alone with his thoughts of vengeance.

And that was how things remained.

Until Ragnarök, that is...

DANISH FOLKTALES

With thought-provoking themes and ideas, these Danish folktales have left me questioning the world as I currently know it. I hope they will do the same for you as you read about an entitled beetle, an anxious fir tree wishing for a better life, and a young boy who proves that not all skills can be studied!

LITTLE THUMBELINA

Among Hans Christian Andersen's earliest tales is "Thumbelina", first published in 1835 as "Tommelise". There have been a number of adaptations of "Thumbelina" featured in films and TV shows around the world, including Russian and Japanese versions. In this tale, a tiny girl meets a marriage-minded toad and mole on her way to finding true love.

Once upon a time, there was an old woman who lived alone in a cottage. She had never had any children, nor did she ever marry. So she took to caring for her garden, giving it all the love and care that a mother would give. But eventually, not even her beloved garden could take away her feeling of loneliness.

One day, as the old woman tended to the fruits of her garden, she was interrupted by a witch coming to visit her.

"Oh my, that's a wonderful garden you've got there! It radiates so much warmth and love."

This witch wore a black dress cinched at the waist and a pointy hat, but she didn't have green skin! She looked nothing like the witches the old woman had read about in books.

"It seems that taking care of a garden is all I'm good for these days," she replied.

The woman and the witch chatted for a long time, the woman teaching the witch all about how to maintain a garden. When the witch spoke of her bodily ailments, the woman went into the house to quickly concoct a drink from the herbs and fruits of her garden that she knew would cure her poorly joints.

"Are you the witch or am I?" the witch quipped before taking a long sip of the drink. "Oh my, I think it's working already!"

The woman smiled to herself, pleased she could take care of someone else for once. "I'm glad I could help you. If only I had children I could look after."

"You don't have any children?"

The woman shook her head. "No. I … am not able to."

The witch did not pry. She could see the hurt in the woman's face by her downturned lips and the way her eyes swiftly became glassy. Instead, the witch retrieved a seed from her pocket and placed it in the woman's hands.

"What's this?" the woman asked.

The witch smiled. "Plant it in your best soil and only water it with the clearest of waters. But before you do any of that…" The witch paused. "Give the seed all your love."

The woman peered at the witch with scepticism but did as she asked.

Once the witch left, the woman found her most beautiful pot and planted the seed using only her finest soil. The next day, she poured fresh rainwater over the plant. For four nights, she watered it and gave it all her love: she spoke to it, she sang to it and she even hugged the plant pot itself.

On the fifth day, a flower had sprouted and the petals had opened, but there was also something the woman never expected to see: a small girl, no larger than a thumb, sitting up and peering at her! She was a beautiful little girl with golden hair that lit up her whole world and who could fit in her palm.

She named her Thumbelina.

The woman provided for Thumbelina a walnut shell, which she used as a bed, and flower petals she could use as a blanket to keep herself warm. She also provided for Thumbelina a teacup in which she could bathe, and handmade all her clothes as even doll dresses were too big for her! Moreover, she taught Thumbelina a song her mother had sung for her decades earlier as well as how to mend her own clothes.

And while the woman cared for Thumbelina, Thumbelina cared for the woman just as much. Each night, Thumbelina would sing the old lady to sleep, her melodic voice inspiring the most wonderful of dreams.

Unfortunately the woman was not the only one who enjoyed Thumbelina's singing. All those times she sang to the woman, a toad out in the garden had been listening in, and on a warm summer night when the tiny girl had fallen asleep, the toad crept through an open window to approach our Thumbelina.

Upon seeing her, the toad was struck by Thumbelina's beauty.

"She'll be perfect for my son!" she cried. Quickly, the toad grabbed Thumbelina's walnut bed and carried her off to a nearby river.

At the river, the toad showed her son Thumbelina, fast asleep. "I have found you a bride!"

The son could not have cared less about Thumbelina. He didn't want a bride – he just wanted to hop around!

But the mother toad ignored her son's lack of excitement and instead placed Thumbelina near a patch of lily pads. She was to rest there until morning, when a house of mud and reeds would be made for the new couple.

Thumbelina awoke hours later in a state of confusion. Where was she? She peered out of her walnut bed and saw that she was resting on a lily pad rather than the windowsill on which her mother usually kept her. Immediately, Thumbelina broke down in tears.

Swimming along the river were two fish who heard Thumbelina's sobs.

"Oh dear. I wonder what's got her so distraught," one of the fish said.

The fish swam to Thumbelina, who could barely get a word out through her sobs.

"I don't know where I am! I must go home! My mother must be so worried about me!"

The two fish looked at one another with determination before they swam over to the stalk and chewed at it until the lily pad came free. Soon, Thumbelina was waving goodbye to her aquatic heroes, her tears drying at the prospect of going home.

Thumbelina travelled for hours, floating away down the river and soaking up all that nature was able to offer her. She watched the sky turn shades of blue while her ears were met with the melody of crickets chirping away and her nostrils were filled with the lovely aroma of flowers that grew at the river's edge. The comfort of nature made Thumbelina feel less afraid of being lost and alone.

As she travelled on, she still could not recognize where was. She realized that she must had been taken further from home than she expected, or the river was taking her in a different direction. Even so, she trusted that the natural world would never lead her down the wrong path.

She would get home, to her mother, one day. And in the meantime, she would soon learn she was never truly alone. At one point, a butterfly joined her on her journey, keeping her company for a short while as she floated along the river. During the summer months, as Thumbelina stopped off at the riverbank, she befriended bees and butterflies. She surrounded herself with nature, bathed in the sun's warm rays and sought shelter under large green leaves, munching on berries she picked from nearby bushes. She filled her mind with new sights and the music of the chirping birds.

But as the seasons changed from summer to autumn, Thumbelina suddenly lost her friends. Her winged companions flew elsewhere, and the sun was no longer as warm as it used to be. Thumbelina's world was suddenly cold, quiet and empty.

It became even worse in winter when the temperatures dropped below anything she had experienced before. How would she ever survive outside without her mother or a house? She couldn't even use the leaves as shelter any more as they were all disappearing underneath the white snow.

One day, when the snow had fallen thick, Thumbelina ventured further than she ever had in search of warmth and sustenance. As she wandered, she came across a meadow where there was a small hole in the earth that she could climb inside before the sun set. When she burrowed inside, she was surprised to find a field mouse!

"Come in. I will allow you to stay here," the mouse said, easing Thumbelina's fear. "But in return, I require your help with the chores."

Thumbelina agreed, and so the mouse and Thumbelina began living together. Although the field mouse was not very friendly to her, whenever Thumbelina sang, his demeanour softened.

One morning, Thumbelina awoke to see the mouse in a panic.

"What's wrong?" she asked.

The mouse stopped scurrying around for a moment. "Our neighbour. He is on his way to visit and he is very important! He's my best friend, Mole."

Thumbelina nodded, but she could sense that was not all the mouse was worrying about.

Later that day, as expected, the mole came to visit. The mouse was nervously watching his interactions with Thumbelina, his teeth chattering more loudly than you'd ever think possible.

"She can sing, you know," the field mouse said quickly. "Voice of an angel!"

"Then you shall sing for me, Thumbelina," the mole instructed. "I may be blind, but you can tell a lot about a person by their voice."

Thumbelina sang to the mole, her voice light as a feather.

"Tell me a story, Thumbelina," the mole demanded.

And so she did, recounting the tale of how she fatefully ended up living in the hole with the mouse.

The mole was mightily impressed by Thumbelina. Her singing and her stories made him feel safe, and he fell in love with her immediately.

After that visit, the mole came over frequently, making excuses to be near Thumbelina. He even invited her to visit his home. Thumbelina was hesitant, for she did not like the mole. Despite their conversations, she found him to be quite vain and uninteresting. Nonetheless, she agreed to visit him if only to keep the field mouse, who had provided for her, happy.

The day she visited the mole, she saw a bird lying in the middle of the tunnel that connected to his home.

"He's dead, leave him be," the mole said. "He can't harm anyone so there's nothing to worry about."

But Thumbelina could see that the bird was not dead. At least, she did not think so. She could see a faint movement of the bird's chest.

"I think he's alive. Are you sure he's not injured?"

The mole looked at her with disdain. "I already told you. He's dead."

"Why don't you move him then?"

The mole waved her question away. "We'll let one of the other moles move him. I'm not the only person responsible for this tunnel!"

After a long and unhappy afternoon spent with the mole, Thumbelina returned to her hole to rest. But she could not relax. All she could think about was the bird in the tunnel. Thumbelina was sure he was still alive. What if he was sick? She had to help him.

Before she could change her mind, she quietly crept through the hole, grabbing a bed sheet before she left, and went back to the tunnel. At the tunnel, she swept up the bird in the sheet and hugged him, hoping what little warmth her body possessed would awaken him.

Suddenly, she heard something.

Lup dup. Lup dup. Lup dup.

It was a heartbeat. She was right! The bird was alive! He was simply too cold to move.

With the help of the field mouse, they moved the bird to the hole and cared for him until he was back in full health. Thumbelina and the bird spent most of their days together, the field mouse far too busy spending time with his friends, and they would often sing to each other. Thumbelina even taught the bird her favourite song, the one her mother had taught her.

When spring came along, the bird asked Thumbelina to travel with him.

"I can't," she said. "I can't leave the field mouse. He has cared so much for me."

The bird understood, bid her farewell and took off. Thumbelina wept as the bird became nothing but a speck in the distance.

One summer afternoon, the field mouse announced that the mole would like to marry Thumbelina.

"What?" She nearly collapsed with shock.

"He wants to marry you and you must accept.

You will live a greater life than you do now, and you will be a great wife for him. And besides, I cannot care for you through another winter. I cannot spare any more food when I hardly have enough for myself. The mole, on the other hand, can."

She didn't even have a chance to protest before the field mouse had rounded up an army of spiders to weave her wedding dress.

Over the following days, Thumbelina was distraught at the idea of becoming a wife to somebody she did not love. She missed her mother more than ever. But what could she do? She did not know how to get back to her mother and she could not survive on her own. Marrying Mole was the only way to survive.

One autumn morning, as Thumbelina was singing her song with tears in her eyes, to her delight, she spotted the wings of the bird she had rescued in the winter.

"Thumbelina!" he called from the sky, before landing next to her. "Why so glum?"

Through her tears Thumbelina told the bird everything.

"Well, no need to fret. You won't need to survive another winter with that mole or mouse, for I will take you to the land of summer! Now, Thumbelina, please would you do the honour of flying with me?"

Thumbelina did not have to think twice. This time she would not reject the bird's offer. They travelled for days until they finally arrived at a large meadow filled with flowers, where the sun was brighter than Thumbelina had seen it for months. The bird dropped Thumbelina on a large pink flower, much like the one she had come from. Then, all of a sudden, from behind one of the petals emerged a man the same size as Thumbelina, wearing a crown. He was scared of the bird but felt at ease as soon as he saw Thumbelina.

"Hi, I'm Thumbelina," she said, holding out her hand.

"Hi, I'm the fairy king," the crowned man said.

For weeks the fairy king and Thumbelina met up in the meadow, happily exchanging stories of their lives for hours on end. Thumbelina told the fairy king all about her walnut shell bed while he told her about how his servants would prepare delicious feasts for him. Thumbelina recounted how her mother used to cover her in petals as a blanket while the fairy king noted how he had gone long and far to visit fairy queens and kings across the country. They traded stories as they wandered the meadows, talking for hours on end as if nobody else existed.

It wasn't long before they fell in love.

"Thumbelina, will you be my queen?" the fairy king asked.

Thumbelina smiled. Unlike the toad who had kidnapped her, or the selfish mole who had made demands, or even the mouse who had only been kind to Thumbelina in exchange for her being his maid, the fairy king had asked her what *she* wanted.

"Of course!" she exclaimed, and the fairy king placed his crown on Thumbelina's head.

Seeing how happy Thumbelina now was, the bird flew away to visit her old home, but he promised to return often.

One day, the bird happened to fly to the old woman's cottage. Perching in a tree in her garden, he sang Thumbelina's song. The old woman instantly recognized the song the bird was chirping and shed a tear. For so long, she had worried about what had become of Thumbelina, but now, hearing her song, she knew her daughter must be alive and well.

While Thumbelina lived happily with the fairy king, the woman rejoiced knowing that if she missed her daughter, she could just go to her window and leave food for the bird so it could come back over time to keep chirping Thumbelina's song.

BLOCKHEAD HANS

In this fairy tale, three brothers, two educated and one not, set out to marry a princess and learn what it means to be truly smart along the way. "Blockhead Hans" was first published in 1855 and there are a number of translations and retellings of the story, including "Clumsy Hans", "Silly Hans" and "Jack the Dullard".

Once upon a time, in a manor in the countryside, lived an old squire with his three sons. The two elder brothers were twice as sharp and clever as their younger brother, who was a little bit foolish and often seemed away with the fairies. The old squire was, of course, incredibly proud of his two elder sons, but he rarely paid any attention to his youngest, who they had come to name Blockhead Hans.

Blockhead Hans, despite his rather cruel nickname, tried his hardest to make his father proud. He read every day, even though it took him twice as long to finish a book as it took his brothers. He worked hard to cook meals for his family, even if he did often get the timing or the ingredients wrong. He even tried to harvest grapes from the vines outside their house, though he would often cut himself with the sickle by accident. Despite Hans's best efforts, his father was still never pleased.

One day, the family heard through the grapevine that the princess of the kingdom was looking to marry. She had noted that she was looking for a suitor who was both brave and funny but also intelligent. Upon hearing this news, the two elder brothers declared that they were going to propose to the princess.

"She'll be mine," one brother announced.

"No, she'll be mine!" the other said.

Although they had much knowledge already, they spent eight days preparing themselves – learning the Latin dictionary by heart, memorizing every single article that had been printed in the town newspaper for the past three years, studying the laws of the guilds and carefully researching current affairs.

On the ninth day, their father gave to each of them a horse that would take them all the way to the princess.

"I believe in you, my sons," the old squire said. "One of you will win the princess's heart, of that I am sure."

The family's servants, who had gathered in their yard to see them off, cheered as the brothers jumped on their horses.

"I will make you all proud," one brother said.

"That's wishful thinking, brother," the other one argued. "We both know she will choose me!"

"But if she doesn't … at least there's me!"

The servants laughed at the two brothers' banter. Just then, Hans woke up from his nap to see all the commotion in the yard.

"What's going on?" he asked as he made his way through the crowd of servants. "Where are you two going? And why are you all dressed up?"

The two brothers rolled their eyes at their younger brother.

"Typical Blockhead Hans! We're going to win the princess's hand in marriage, obviously," one brother said.

"Oh," Hans replied. That would explain all the studying they had been doing for the past eight days, he supposed. "Well, I must come, too!"

The two brothers simply laughed at Hans before riding away on their quest.

Hans turned to his father. "Father, may I borrow a horse? I must go with them!"

The old squire shook his head. "Forget it, Blockhead Hans. Why would you go? It would be for nothing!"

"You don't know that," said Hans. "She might take a liking to me. And then we could get married!"

The old squire was getting frustrated with his son. Well, even more frustrated than normal, that is.

"There's no point. She won't choose you! She will have many impressive suitors, and you don't have what she is looking for. You are not smart, brave or funny. Your brothers, on the other hand, are!"

"But Father, please!"

The old squire was getting tired arguing with his son. "If you want to go, you'll have to find your own way!"

Hans watched as his father went back inside, ignoring his pleas for help. His shoulders sagged in disappointment.

"Fine. If he won't spare me a horse, I'll just have to..." Hans was looking around for something that could transport him, when his eyes landed on the animal only a few feet away from him. "The goat! I'll go on the goat! It will carry me just as well as a horse would!"

The goat looked up with horror in its eyes. It was safe to say that it was not pleased about being the chosen one!

"Here I come!" Hans announced as he sat on the goat and kicked his heels in its sides. The goat's legs sprang into action and it rushed along the highway as if it truly were a horse. Perhaps it had been hiding its potential all along – or perhaps it wanted to end its suffering as quickly as it could!

Despite the speed of the goat's legs, the brothers

on horseback had a head start. But Hans knew a shortcut to the palace, and he quickly took the path that led him towards the mountain.

On the way, he found something lying in the middle of the path.

"What's this?" he asked. He jumped off the goat to investigate the mound of black feathers. "Ah, it's a crow! Perhaps I shall take it to the princess. I'm sure she will find some use for it!"

The goat's eyes widened with alarm. *Why* did Hans think a dead crow would be something a *princess* would like? Unfortunately, things did not get any better as the journey went on. Along the way Hans also picked up other gifts: an old wooden shoe and a ball of slimy mud.

Passing over the mountain, Hans finally caught up with his brothers.

"Hello!" he shouted, riding up behind them. "I made it!"

The two brothers turned, their jaws dropping. "What are you doing here, Blockhead Hans?"

"Well, I'm off to see the princess, just like you!"

"Seriously, *you* are going to try to compete for the princess's affection?" one brother asked.

"Of course! Why not?" said Hans.

"For one, you're riding on a goat rather than a fine horse!" said one brother.

"And let's not forget you're not exactly smart either!" the other brother said with a laugh.

"Well, I have something you don't," Hans told his brothers before digging into his satchel and pulling out his treasures – the dead crow, the wooden shoe and the ball of mud. "I think she'll like them!"

The brothers did not think Hans's so-called "treasures" even warranted a response. Instead, they snorted, rolled their eyes and kicked their horses onward at a gallop, leaving Hans behind.

At the castle, a long line had already formed. There, every suitor was given a number and then told to wait before they were called in one by one.

Hans was at least an hour behind, hobbling along slowly on his exhausted goat, while the older brothers took their places with the rest of the townsfolk. They stood close to the castle's windows, watching as the princess rejected suitors left, right and centre.

"No good!" The princess would shout. "Get out before I have you thrown out!"

The once confident brothers grew concerned about their chances.

"Perhaps she's asking them some really difficult questions," one brother suggested.

"Maybe so. But we are wholly prepared! We'll surely do better than Blockhead Hans!" the other brother said.

By the time Hans arrived, the line had shortened and only a handful of suitors remained. Hans was not worried by the princess's rejections. Instead, he was more concerned about feeding the goat after such long and tiring travels.

"Thank you for taking me all the way here." Hans patted the goat's head gratefully. "Please rest and eat as much grass as you wish!"

The goat obliged without a second thought.

After another hour, the brothers' turns came to see the princess.

When the first brother stepped into the room, he forgot all that he had planned to say: all the words from the dictionary he had memorized, along with all the laws he had studied, seemed to fall from his brain. He tried to buy himself time by moving about in place, but the creaking floorboards put him off. He was feeling unnerved by the three reporters who stood around him and wrote down everything that was said, or *not* being said, so that it could be printed in the newspaper the following day. It certainly didn't help either that the room was terribly hot!

"Well, have you got anything to say to me?" the princess prompted.

"Well, uh, it's as warm as a Finnish sauna in here," the brother said.

"It's only natural," the princess responded. "I am roasting chickens today after all!"

The brother was at a loss for words, taken aback by how casually the princess had spoken to him.

"Ugh, you've got nothing to say, do you? Get out!" the princess demanded. At the princess's dismissal, a servant escorted the brother out.

Only a moment later, the other brother stepped in. He wasn't as intimidated as his brother and remarked on the temperature of the room right away.

"It's terribly hot in here, isn't it?"

"Of course it is, I am roasting chickens today after all!" the princess said, repeating to him what she had told his brother.

And, just like his brother, her suitor was at a loss for words. It seemed his nerves had caught up with him, and he wasn't sure how to respond. "Pardon?"

"Ugh, you're not the one either. Nothing to say for yourself. Why will nobody speak to me like a normal person? Get out!"

The servant escorted the second brother out before he even had a chance to process what the princess had said.

Finally, it was Hans's turn. "Hello, my dear princess! I must say, it's burning in here!"

Again, the princess said, "As it should be. I am roasting chickens here today after all!"

Without missing a beat, Hans pulled out the dead crow from his satchel. "Oh, how lovely! Shall we roast my crow as well?"

The princess was surprised by Hans's quick, funny response and gave a delighted laugh. "Certainly. Though I haven't got any pots or pans to roast it in. Unless you do?"

"I certainly do!" Hans pulled out the wooden shoe from his bag and placed the crow inside it. "I'm sorry about the smell, but it ought to do as a vessel to roast the crow! What do you think, Princess?"

The princess thought for a moment. "That's a great idea. We would have a whole meal if only we had gravy for the crow. I'm sure you don't have that, do you?"

"Oh, but I do! I found so much on my travels. A benefit of riding on a goat and not a horse, I guess – a little closer to the ground!" Hans reached into his pocket and pulled out the slimy ball of mud. "Here's our gravy! We can simply marinate the crow by rubbing it into the feathers like this..."

To the reporters' surprise, Hans went over and rubbed the mud into the servant's face – which made the princess laugh so much her stomach ached.

She couldn't help but like Hans. He spoke to her freely and treated her normally. What's more, he was brave enough to ride all this way on a goat, smart enough to use items for purposes other than those they were intended for and, perhaps most importantly, he could make her laugh!

"You're just what I'm looking for," the princess said. "I will marry you!"

And so "Blockhead Hans" became king – proving to his brothers, father and everybody else that some skills cannot be studied, and that we all have qualities that will be recognized by somebody.

THE BEETLE

"The Beetle" was first published in 1861, written by acclaimed author Hans Christian Andersen. This is a tale that offers both humour and fantasy, with a message about not being greedy and knowing that good things come to those who wait!

Once upon a time, there was an emperor, and he shod his favourite horse with golden shoes. It might sound odd to use such an expensive material on an animal, but *this* horse had once saved the emperor's life. When a cow had loomed towards the emperor, about to trample him, the horse had kicked the cow away. For this, the emperor was forever grateful and promised to do his utmost to take care of the horse and treat him like royalty.

Not everybody thought it was fair for the horse to receive such nice things. Living in one of the stables was a beetle who thought he, too, should be rewarded. Why? Because he felt strongly that greatness comes in many forms and sizes – and the beetle was determined to prove just that.

One day, he crawled to visit the farrier – the blacksmith who shod the emperor's horses.

"Excuse me," said the beetle.

"What is it you want?" the farrier asked.

Without missing a beat, the beetle replied, "Golden shoes, of course."

The farrier laughed in the beetle's face. "Get out of here."

"Why? If the horse can have golden shoes, surely so can I?" said the beetle.

The farrier shook his head. "Not happening."

"Am I not as good as the horse? I do live in the same stable!" the beetle argued.

"Listen, the horse has earned his golden shoes. He did not receive them for simply living in the stable," the farrier reasoned.

The beetle harrumphed. "Well then, I guess I'll be leaving the stable altogether to find my *own* fortune."

The farrier snorted. "You do that, my friend. But remember, the horse is special. There is a reason he was given those shoes."

"I am not your friend; for a friend would have given me my shoes! And I am special, too!" the beetle cried as he exited the stable and flew away from where he did not feel appreciated.

The beetle used his wings to fly to a flower garden where he knew the ladybirds lived.

"Ah, have you come to smell my flowers?" one of the ladybirds asked him as she flew from flower to flower with her delicate wings. "Oh, they're even sweeter today than they were yesterday, and they are looking even more beautiful in the radiant sunshine!"

The beetle frowned. "I've seen better things. I

mean, there isn't even a dung heap here! No, this will not do for me."

The beetle carried on travelling until he came to a great haystack, beneath which a caterpillar lived.

"Gosh, I cannot get over how amazing the world is! I mean, can you *feel* the sun. Isn't it just the right temperature today?" The caterpillar closed its eyes and tilted its head to catch the rays of the sun. "I cannot wait to go to sleep and wake up as a gorgeous butterfly who can fly with ravishing wings. Oh, just imagine all the things I will see. So much greatness stands before me!"

"Ha!" the beetle scoffed. "There's nothing all that great about flying! I've got wings and nothing wonderful has ever happened to me. Just thinking about it angers me, and I do not want to be angry so I shall fly away – at least my wings grant me that one simple pleasure!"

The beetle flew away. Shortly after, he landed on a large lawn. There, he took shelter from the rain that had just begun to fall, hiding in a pillowcase that had been placed on a line to dry. The cotton was still slightly damp and certainly not as nice as the stable he had grown accustomed to, but it would have to make do while it was still raining.

To his surprise, when he awoke hours later, he found two frogs with him in the pillowcase!

"Oh, this weather is absolutely tropical!" said one frog.

"Isn't it just? The dampness reminds me of lying in a wet ditch, and I haven't had that pleasure for months now! I hope it stays this way for quite some time!" said the other.

The beetle crawled over to the two frogs, feeling the need to interject. "This weather is nothing but horrid. Have you ever been in the emperor's stable?"

The two frogs stared at the beetle in response. He took that as to mean they hadn't.

"Well, *there* the dampness isn't cold but warm and cosy. This weather is nothing but a nuisance and I must get out of here! Tell me, do you know where the nearest dung heap is? I need to take up a new home and a dung heap is the next best thing after the comforts of the emperor's stable."

But the frogs simply shook their head, not wanting to engage further with the beetle. Annoyed, the beetle left the pillowcase and dropped down to the lawn, which was now covered in drops of rain. He crawled his way over to a broken piece of pottery which would cover him until the bad weather subsided.

There, he found a family of earwigs. He had heard good things of earwigs – the female figures were known to be maternal and full of affection for their children and visitors. He was certain they would respond to his query unlike the frogs.

"Tell me, where can I find the nearest dung heap?" he inquired.

"Oh, my darling, you will find it on the other side of the ditch," said one of the earwigs.

And so the beetle flew to the ditch, where he met several other beetles.

"Welcome to our home," they said upon seeing him, instantly recognizing him as one of their own. "You look tired. Are you tired? Oh, come on in!"

"I certainly am. You see, I have been travelling a long way. I have been exposed to rain and now I am very clean, which I am not very fond of. But I must say, standing here with you, companions of my own kind, I suddenly feel a little better."

The beetles smiled at him and nursed him back to health, the youngsters tending to his tired, sore wings.

"You know," said the mother beetle, "none of my daughters are engaged yet."

The young female beetles giggled in embarrassment.

"Well, they certainly are beautiful," the beetle said. "Your eldest daughter especially."

The eldest daughter looked away with a bashful smile.

"Well, I give you my blessing to marry her!"

With the blessing of the mother, the beetle married the eldest daughter the very next day. There was no reason to delay the wedding.

The beetle was comfortable in his new home with his new wife, but after three days he decided to leave as he needed to gather food and drink for his new family.

"They have taken me in and now it is my turn to take care of them," he told himself before flying away.

The beetle sailed across the ditch in only a cabbage leaf, his journey long and arduous. On his way, two people loomed over the ditch and, to the beetle's alarm, they bent to pick him up, intrigued by the sight of him. They translated the beetle's name into Latin, discussing its origin and history.

"Shall we carry him home? He would make the most wonderful specimen for our research!" one man asked his companion.

"No, I have places to be!" the beetle cried. He quickly flew out of the man's hand, escaping their clutches, and soon after found himself inside a greenhouse.

"Ooh, look at all these plants I can feast on once they rot! And the temperature, it's just divine in here." The beetle lay down, dreaming of how one day the emperor would give him golden shoes, when he was rudely awakened by somebody seizing his body once again.

This time a young boy turned him round and round, inspecting him. "Hello, friend. Let's play, shall we?"

The young boy wrapped the beetle in a vine leaf before putting him in his pocket. The beetle attempted to escape by scraping the insides of the boy's trousers but failed miserably. If anything, it aggravated the young boy and caused him to give the beetle a gentle squeeze as an order to keep still. After some time, the boy went to the lake and put the beetle on a broken wooden shoe, tying him to a stick with some thread.

"Now you are a sailor," the boy said before pushing the wooden shoe on to the lake.

The beetle was scared. While the lake wasn't a

large one to a human, it felt like a vast ocean to the beetle.

"This is it, isn't it?" the beetle sighed. "First, I am refused the golden shoes. Now I am tied to a mast, at the mercy of violent waves. If only I had been given my shoes, I wouldn't be here! The currents will seize me, take my life and nobody will ever hear of the adventures I've been on. But perhaps that is just as well. People do not seem to understand my worth anyway."

Just as the beetle was resigning himself to his fate, two young girls came rowing up in a boat.

"Oh look, there's a creature tied to the wooden shoe!" said one girl.

"Let's check it out," said the other.

They came closer to the wooden shoe, investigating the beetle and his "boat" before fishing it out of the water altogether. One of the girls drew a small pair of scissors from her pocket and cut the thread holding the beetle to the mast.

"Fly," whispered the girl.

And the beetle did not need telling twice. He flew up and up, and through a window of the first building he saw.

He was so exhausted that it took him a moment

to realize he was back in the emperor's favourite stable – and in fact he had landed on the emperor's favourite horse. He clung to the horse's mane and sat there for some time, recovering from his adventure.

"Huh, here I am sitting on the emperor's favourite horse, just like the emperor himself!" The beetle smiled, remembering what the farrier had said – that the horse was special, and there was a reason he was given those golden shoes. "Perhaps it was always known that one day I would take the emperor's place and ride his horse… Maybe that is why the horse was given the golden shoes in the first place! Yes, that is the only possible explanation."

The beetle, pleased with the outcome of things, finally understood how that one moment had helped him. If the farrier hadn't made him so angry and denied his request for the golden shoes, he would never have gone on his journey and ended up right here on the horse's mane, convinced of his worth.

"Travelling truly does expand your mind," he said to himself as he lay on the horse's mane, the rays of the sun shining upon him through the windows. "And one ought to remember there is always a reason for the order of things."

THE GOBLIN AND THE GROCER

This tale is about a goblin who must choose between poetry and his Christmas jam. Hans Christian Andersen first published "The Goblin and the Grocer" in 1852, and it is actually inspired by his own life – his first publication barely paid a dime, and his poetry book pages were ripped out and used as cheese wrappings!

Once upon a time, a hard-working but poor student lived in a small room on the top floor of a house owned by a grocer, Mr Jensen, who was equally hard-working but had much more to show for it. Mr Jensen's shop was on the ground floor, and he lived on the first floor with his wife, Mrs Jensen, and a household goblin.

The goblin had nothing of his own and was very happy to stick by Mr Jensen. Mr Jensen could afford to provide the luxury of a warm bed and piping-hot food that tickled all the senses. Plus, every Christmas Eve, the goblin received his favourite treat: a piece of sourdough slathered with tasty jam. A free room and food – what more could he ask for?

One evening, the student came down to the shop to buy some candles and cheese. As he wandered the aisles, he couldn't help but wonder what it might be like to one day be able to purchase all the things he truly wanted, rather than the bare minimum he had budgeted for. He could only dream of it, and dreams were not something he could afford. Dreams did not, after all, pay the bills.

"Lovely day today, isn't it? I hope you're getting on well with your studies. Got everything you were looking for? We've got some ham that could go well with that cheese, you know," Mrs Jensen chattered as the student handed his items over to Mr Jensen, who stood next to her. Mrs Jensen was very friendly and so talkative it could be hard to get a word in edgeways. "We've also got some flavoursome butter that would be excellent to slather on your potatoes!"

"Ah, nothing else for me, thank you," the student responded as he paid the grocers. After untangling himself from the conversation with Mrs Jensen, who still had many questions for him, he said goodbye to the couple and made his way to his attic room.

On his way, he suddenly stopped still. His cheese was wrapped in paper, which was not uncommon, but he noticed that it was not wrapped in plain paper, or even newspaper. Rather, it appeared to have been wrapped in a page from an old book. More specifically, a book of poetry.

Why would anyone ever use poetry to wrap cheese? Poetry was far too beautiful and important to be used as wrapping!

The student turned back and found Mr Jensen and the goblin organizing some shelves. Mr Jensen was restocking some apples while the goblin tidied a box of newspapers.

"Where did you get this?" the student asked, gesturing to the paper.

Mr Jensen frowned. "The wrapping? An old woman traded in an old book of poetry for some coffee earlier this week. If you want the rest of the pages, I can give it to you for two pence."

The student looked down at the block of cheese. He so wanted to read more of the poetry and save the book from the sad fate of being torn up to wrap around food, but money was tight. "How about I give you the cheese back? That should equate to the same amount."

"You're sure?" said Mr Jensen in surprise. "Your bread will be rather dull without cheese."

"I'm sure. But I would much rather eat plain bread than see a book torn to pieces, especially a poetry book. To think that to you, a practical man, art is nothing but something to wrap around cheese! Why, I think you understand as much about poetry as that box of newspapers does!"

Now you might think that the student was being a little rude to Mr Jensen, but the grocer only laughed in good humour because he knew it was a joke. Even so, the goblin could not help but feel angry. How dare the student say such a thing? Mr

Jensen owned the house the student slept in and sold the items he consumed. Surely he should have been respectful, rather than insulting the grocer's intelligence! Not only that, the goblin thought, but his comment could even be said to offend the box of newspapers, too. The goblin remained quiet, but the thought continued to play on his mind.

That night, once the shop had shut and Mr and Mrs Jensen had gone to sleep, the goblin crept to their room on the first floor. Using his strange magic, the goblin was able to borrow the tongue of the talkative Mrs Jensen without her even stirring. She had no use for it while she was asleep after all, and he would restore it before she woke. The goblin was used to borrowing her tongue, for he had used it before to turn any object that could not previously speak into a chatterbox, their thoughts and feelings finally allowed to roam free. Fortunately for him, he could only use the tongue on one item at a time, otherwise his ears would have been assaulted by too many voices!

The goblin silently sneaked downstairs and laid the tongue on the box in which Mr Jensen kept the newspapers. Within a few seconds, the box came to life.

"Hello!" it said, a little louder than the goblin anticipated.

"Shhh," the goblin whispered. "Not too noisy. You wouldn't want Mr Jensen to wake up, would you? Or Mrs Jensen to discover her tongue is being used by someone else!"

"Sorry, friend! I'll keep it down. Now how can I help?"

"Did you hear what the student said earlier?" asked the goblin.

"Oh yes, I heard him all right," the box said, a hint of annoyance in his voice.

"Is it true? Do you not know anything about poetry?"

"It is not true, Goblin. Poetry is sometimes in the papers. They stick it at the end when they've run out of stories to report on, and I've seen *plenty* of poems in my time. In fact, I'd say I know a great deal more about poetry than that student in the attic, even though I am nothing but a box in Mr and Mrs Jensen's shop. And, if you ask me, that student is a fool. I would never have traded food for poetry!"

Then the goblin put the tongue on other items one by one – the coffee mill, the butter cask, the sack of flour – asking each of them, "What do you know about poetry?"

And each item responded similarly to the box: they knew that poetry was simply a string of words thrown in at the end of the newspaper when there was nothing else to write about.

"It's not worth anything!" said the coffee mill.

"It doesn't provide anything," said the butter cask.

"Whereas *we* provide goods that give people their fill," said the sack of flour.

"Well then, I shall let the student know that he is not as clever as he thinks he is and that he shouldn't have spoken to the master the way he did!"

After silently returning the tongue to Mrs Jensen, the goblin crept up the stairs to the attic where the student lived, his footsteps soft so as to not make the steps creak. Through the keyhole, the goblin could see that the candle was still burning in the room and that the student was poring over the torn book he had exchanged his cheese for earlier.

The student softly read the words aloud, and the goblin was shocked to find them beautiful. In fact, the book seemed to brighten the room even more than the candle did, shooting a streak of light from its pages. As the student recited the words of a poem, the light cast across the ceiling appeared to the goblin like a tree. If he angled himself well enough, he could see dancing leaves, each one vibrant, a spread of twinkling stars and delicate flowers. Along with the light, gentle music seemed to play throughout the room. The goblin was in awe, until finally the student blew out the candle to go to sleep.

"Wow," the goblin said to himself. "That was … beautiful! He was right about poetry. I must come and stay with the student!"

But as soon as he said it, he realized he couldn't. The student had barely any money! Through the keyhole, the goblin could see that he had very few belongings, and ate little more than plain bread. How would he provide the goblin with his beloved Christmas Eve sourdough and jam?

The night passed, and the goblin worked in the shop with the grocer the next day, yet he itched to be near the student's room again, to feel the warmth and hear the sweet melody of the poetry he read.

He waited until the couple had again gone to sleep before heading in the direction of the student's room. He peeked through the keyhole, listening to the student read, and was once again swept up in the feeling of warmth from something he could not yet name. Silently, the goblin burst into tears. He could not explain them, but all he knew was that they were not sad but happy.

At the same time, he was a tad jealous of the student. He dreamed of how glorious it would be to sit with a book of poetry and feel its burst of energy. Instead, he had to eavesdrop through the other side of the door. The landing where he stood was cold, an icy draught freezing him in place, but the goblin did not feel it, at least until the light through the keyhole went out and the poetry's song died down. With the book now shut, the goblin crept down to his much warmer corner of the house and slept, pretending to be content with what he had.

Soon enough, Christmas came around, and he was met with his usual sourdough slathered with mouth-watering jam. As always, the Jensens provided for him, and he was grateful.

Then one night, only a few days after Christmas, the goblin was awoken by a commotion outside – people hammering on the door and shouting. Was that the smell of smoke? Then the watchman blasted his horn! It could only mean one thing … a great fire had broken out. When the goblin looked out of the window, he could see the whole street in flames! He didn't know where the fire had started, but it was moving quickly.

Mrs Jensen was panicking when she crossed paths with the goblin.

"Where is my purse? No, that's not what I want – where is my necklace? No, where are my earrings?" Mrs Jensen's questions flew out of her mouth without a sense of direction. "Quick, gather what you can!"

She took her gold earrings from her jewellery box and put them in her pocket for safekeeping as she bustled out of the house. Meanwhile, Mr Jensen ran down to the shop to save his ledger.

"What are you doing?" the goblin asked him.

"Saving my most valuable possession, of course!" Mr Jensen responded. "Now quickly, we must leave before we are engulfed in flames!"

"Where is the student?" the goblin asked.

"He's already out!" Mr Jensen called.

The goblin knew he should run to safety and leave everything behind, but he was seized by the urge to grab *his* most valuable possession. Had the student left it behind? The goblin leaped upstairs and raced to the student's room, where he snatched the torn book of poetry and clutched it to his chest. He had saved the greatest treasure!

The goblin dashed out of the house, joining the grocers and the student outside. There he could see that it was the neighbour's house that was burning. Watching the flames dance, the goblin held on tightly to the book. As the fire was put out and his fear faded away, he realized it was clear what his heart truly valued and with whom he really belonged. This moment had proven that his real love was for poetry, and that he should leave Mr Jensen and live with the student.

But as reality sunk in, the goblin thought again, looking from the student to the couple. "Poetry can only get me so far. It may nourish my soul, but it cannot feed me or provide shelter for me."

The goblin was torn. He wanted the fulfilment that came with the words in the student's book, but he also wanted the comfort that came with living with Mr Jensen.

In the end, he made a decision.

"I will split myself between them. I will spend half of my time with the student, dedicating myself to poetry, and half committed to Mr and Mrs Jensen, eating my jam!"

And it is easy to understand the goblin's struggle. We humans, too, often find it hard to strike the balance between the passions that make us feel alive and what allows us to make a living.

THE FIR TREE

In this tale, an anxious fir tree can't appreciate the moment because he's so eager for growth and greater things. Sometimes we don't know what we've got until it's gone, and this story reminds us of the importance of being grateful for the present. This story was first published in 1844, written by Hans Christian Andersen.

Once upon a time, in a forest far, far away, there stood a fir tree anxious to grow up. It basked in the warm sunshine and was surrounded by fresh air, but the fir tree simply did not care for any of it! It despised being so little. It certainly did not enjoy it when children would pass by and comment on its size as they picked berries from nearby bushes to fill their buckets.

"Oh, look at that tree! Isn't it so nice and small?"

"It's the baby of the woods!"

"How petite and quaint that tree is!"

The fir tree growled – not that they could hear him – and cried, "I hate being little!"

The next year, even with a long joint of new growth, the fir tree couldn't help but sigh. He was still *so* little compared to the tall pines around him.

"All I want is to be a grown-up tree. Then I could see the view from up high and the birds would want to make a home out of my branches. I could even bow back and forth a great distance as the wind blows my way. Oh, there's so much to do when you're all grown up!"

The following winter, even though he had grown yet another joint of new growth, he was still miserable – especially as a hare would often come hopping along and jump past the lower branches of the fir tree as if he were nothing.

It was only two winters later, when he had grown to a medium-sized tree, that the hare could no longer jump over the lower branches of the tree but had to hop around it. The fir tree was satisfied with the development.

"See, this is what happens when you grow. You get taller! And isn't that the most wonderful thing in the world?"

But in the autumn of the next year, the fir tree saw how woodcutters came through the forest and cut down the largest of the trees. He watched in horror as the trees crashed to the ground with their limbs lopped off. He trembled as he watched the naked trunks get loaded into carts and driven away from the forest. He did not understand where they were going – and he did not find out until springtime, when the swallows and storks gave him company.

"Do you know where the older trees have gone?" he asked them.

"Oh yes. Many of them travelled across the seas as tall, stately masts on ships," the stork said. "Some have even gone as far as Egypt! At least I think those are the trees you speak of, for they smelled just like you, like fir."

The fir tree was no longer upset about the disappearance of his friends. Instead, he was excited! When he grew up, he, too, could travel on the seas and see the world. "Oh, I wish I were old *now*!"

"Life is short, my friend," said the sun, who had overheard the conversation. "Do not wish your life away, but take pride in your life now!"

The fir tree ignored the sun. What did she know about life down here on Earth?

When Christmas time came, just like in the spring, many of the trees were cut down and taken away. The fir tree hoped he would be one of them, but alas he was left behind.

"I don't understand. Why aren't they coming for me? I am now much bigger than they are! And why were their branches not cut off like my elders?" he asked.

"We can answer that!" a sparrow chirped. "They're allowed to keep their branches for they are to be decked out in homes!"

"They are not becoming masts on ships?" said the fir tree.

"Oh no, not at all. You wouldn't believe what I've seen through house windows! They are planted in the middle of a warm room where golden and silver apples decorate their branches and boxes are hidden underneath them. Oh, and there are candles everywhere, *so* many candles!"

The fir tree listened in awe. "Such lucky trees! That's even better than travelling the seas as a mast. I wish *I* could be planted in a home just like them!"

"Careful what you wish for," the wind whispered to the tree. "Do not waste your youth wishing when you could enjoy what is already out here in the open, right now."

But the tree did not listen to the wind. Instead, he dreamed of the day when he would be taken away from the forest. He grew and grew until his branches turned a dark evergreen colour that people were unable to ignore come the following winter.

Soon enough, the same men who had taken away the smaller trees came for him.

"Finally," the tree sighed in relief. But just as quickly as the relief appeared, it faded. the tree felt faint with pain, and sadness filled him at the idea of leaving the only home he had known for so many years. Even with many of his comrades having long since left, he was upset that he would be leaving the grounds he had grown up in, and the other trees, plants and animals he had come to know.

The tree was quite miserable until he was unloaded into a yard where a young lad spotted him and said, "Oh, that's a splendid tree. Can we have that one, Father?"

"Yes, you are right," his father replied. "It is quite magnificent."

The tree smiled, and then two servants came to transport him. Eventually he was carried inside a drawing room, where he was planted in a large pot that was wrapped in a green cloth. Around him, there were portraits hung up on the walls, and sofas covered with fuzzy blankets. Across from him, there were tables strewn with all kinds of items: picture books, toys and food.

He couldn't have been any happier if he tried.

The servants hung cut-out coloured paper and silver apples from his branches while candles and walnuts were tied to his twigs. At the very top of the tree they placed a large golden star that made the fir tree so beautiful he felt giddy.

"Oh, this tree will shine so brightly tonight!" the servants exclaimed.

"I cannot wait," the tree thought to himself. "I wonder what I will look like when the candles are lit. Will the other trees try to peer through the windows to see me? And what will happen after tonight? Will I take root in this room for the rest of the year?"

There was so much the tree did not know, but he had nobody to ask. The humans could not hear him like the animals and the sun and the wind could.

When the candles were lit, the tree was surprised at the heat. He quivered, accidentally setting one of his own twigs ablaze.

"Oh no!" he cried out in surprise while the young servant put out the fire quickly. After that, the tree was afraid to move again. What if he had dropped one of the ornaments? How disappointed he would be!

Later, a group of children stormed the room. They all looked at the tree in admiration, and the tree felt so proud at their reaction. But only moments later they forgot all about him as they grabbed for the presents that lay underneath his branches.

"Is that it? Will they pay me no more attention?" he asked.

And it seemed they wouldn't. They were wholly occupied by their presents and the songs that played throughout the house. They danced and played, not once looking at the tree. The tree sighed with disappointment.

"Tell us a story!" the children asked of their father.

The man sat down in his chair with the children at his feet and told them the story of Brother Jacob. As the children listened, the fir tree stood very still and wondered what tomorrow would bring. Perhaps they would decorate him again, perhaps with fruits and the toys the children had received rather than those already hanging on his branches today? The tree dreamed of tomorrow, and when the maid came in the following morning with a duster, he smiled.

"Ah, yes, they have come to renew my beauty," he thought to himself.

But they did not dust him. Instead they dragged him upstairs and left him in a dark corner of the attic where no sunlight ever filtered through.

"Why am I here? How am I to bring the family joy if I am hidden away?"

The tree leaned against the wall, waiting to be remembered. Sometimes, people would come upstairs but only to leave boxes in the corner with him. Not once did they come to say hello or take care of him.

The fir tree thought that perhaps he had not been forgotten but simply put in the attic until the earth outside would thaw enough for them to replant him outside in the garden.

"They are doing this for my own good. They wouldn't want me to freeze after all. Oh, they are lovely people this family! Though I do wish it weren't so lonely or dark in here."

Just then, two mice crept across the floor towards the fir tree.

"Gosh, it's cold in here, isn't it?" squeaked one mouse.

"It certainly is," the other mouse said before they both rustled in and out of the branches. "Other than the cold, it's nice here, isn't it, old fir tree?"

"Who are you calling old?" the fir tree asked. "I will have you know that there are many older trees than me."

"Really? Tell us everything!" squeaked the mouse.

"Yes, tell us where you've been, old fir tree! Where have you been?" asked the other.

"I come from the forest, where the birds sing and the sun shines brightly upon you," he told the mice and began to recount his youthful days in the forest. He even told them about the hare that used to annoy him when he was little, which now he felt strangely nostalgic about. When he was done, the mice looked up at him with giant smiles.

"You must have been so happy in the forest!"

"Compared to here, I guess so, yes," the fir tree said with a slight sadness.

"Where else have you been?" a mouse asked.

"Well, I have been a Christmas tree downstairs. You should have seen how they decked me out with candles and silver apples!"

The fir tree told the mice all about the children and their toys. He told them all about the warmth of the candles and the smells of the food that were prepared.

"Oh, what a wonderful life you have lived!" the mice said.

"I am still living. I have simply stopped growing for the moment, that's all," said the fir tree.

The next night, the two mice brought along four others and some rats, too, who all came to hear what else the tree had to say. Again, the tree recalled its youthful days and its time downstairs.

"Have you got any more stories to tell?" the mice asked him.

The tree thought about it. He had no personal stories to tell, but he could remember the story he heard the father tell his children on Christmas Eve.

"I could tell you the story of Brother Jacob," he offered.

"Yes, please!" the mice and rats called out in unison.

So the fir tree told them all the story of Brother Jacob to the best of his recollection. When he finished, one of the mice asked, "Is that the only story you know?".

"That is indeed," he answered.

"Well then, we are off, and we won't come back for we want *new* stories," one of the rats said, and the mice followed not long after.

When they had all left, the tree sighed. "It was nice to have company, however long it lasted."

Finally, spring came, and the servants were ready to move the tree out of the attic and into the daylight.

"Now my life will start again!" the tree said to

himself. "I knew they hadn't forgotten about me! Hopefully they will take me somewhere outdoors."

He was dragged through the doors and out into the garden, where flowers were blooming and trees were blossoming.

"How wonderful the sun and wind feel out here. I cannot wait to live again," the fir tree rejoiced, trying to stretch out his branches. But as he did, he realized in the light of day that they were all withered and brown. Then he was tossed into a corner of the garden among the weeds and nettles!

"Oh look," said the children who were not far away from him. "It's our old Christmas tree. It's even got the star on top! Daddy must have forgotten to remove it!"

The young boy trampled over the fir tree, the brittle branches cracking underneath his feet, until he could pluck the star off it. The tree yelped in disappointment.

"They didn't care for me at all! They only made me look all gorgeous to suit *their* party." The tree cried to himself. "Oh, how I wish I hadn't grown up. If I were young, I would still be in the forest with the sun and the wind and the other trees and the animals – those who actually appreciated me!

Why did I take it all for granted? Why did I not listen to my wise elders and hold on to my youth while I could?"

Before the fir tree could ruminate further over his poor decisions, the servant came with an axe. Then the fir tree was chopped up – not to be made into a mast like some of his old friends, but to be heaped into a pile for a bonfire.

As the tree was set ablaze and turned into smoke, he could not help but remember his bright summer days and starlit nights in the forest. If he could, he would go back and tell his younger self to stop wishing his life away, when he could simply have lived in the present.

NORWEGIAN FOLKTALES

With their cunning nature, these Norwegian folktales often made me laugh. I hope they have the same effect on you as you read about a brave little goat crossing a bridge where a troll dwells, a fox going to extreme lengths for a stick of butter around Christmas time and a daughter seeking revenge!

THE SQUIRE'S BRIDE

In this story, a young woman is promised by her father to a man she does not want to marry – and tricks everyone to escape her unwanted fate. Folktales such as this one were published in Peter Christen Asbjørnsen and Jørgen Moe's wonderful nineteenth-century Norwegian collection titled Norske Folkeeventyr.

Once upon a time, there was a squire with more fortune and land than he could wish for. He owned a large farm and a beautiful home, but there was one thing the squire did not have that he so desperately wanted: a wife.

One day, as he pondered on how to find a woman to marry, he noticed someone working away in the nearby hayfield. He wandered closer to where the woman was working and was instantly taken aback by her beauty. Her long brown hair framed her face perfectly, her cheeks were flushed with colour, and as she worked, she sang to herself with a beautiful voice.

As she looked up, the squire realized it was his neighbour's daughter! He did not know much about the neighbours, but he did know that they did not have an awful lot of money – which meant marrying him, a rich man, would be an offer the woman wouldn't be able to refuse.

"Can I help you?" she asked the squire, shielding her eyes from the sun.

"Why, yes, I think you can." The squire smoothed down his hair as he made his way over to her. "I've been thinking I want to marry."

"That's good for you that you are able to think," she quipped with a sly smile.

The squire was not dissuaded. "Yes, it is, for I've been thinking that I want to marry *you*."

"Ah, well, I think you should keep thinking in that case," the young woman said.

"What? You don't want to marry me?"

The woman sighed as if the conversation drained her. "That is exactly what I am saying. Though I am honoured you thought of me."

And with that, she carried on working, not giving the squire another thought. The squire stood silently for a moment, sure she would change her mind, for he was not used to people refusing his offers – but she didn't. And the more she ignored him, the more determined he was to marry her.

The next day, the squire went to see the young woman's father.

"I'm sorry, sir, but I still don't have the money," the old man said to the squire as soon as they had both sat down.

"Oh yes – your debt," said the squire. A few years back, the old man had borrowed some funds to pay for the farm machinery he needed, promising he would repay him as soon as he could. Unfortunately for the old man, he had made no more money than before. The squire now realized this could be very convenient for him. "How about, instead of a monetary payment, you repay me by convincing your daughter to marry me instead?"

The old man hesitated. It was an offer he truly couldn't resist. But could he convince his daughter to marry somebody she barely even knew?

"And," the squire continued, "I'll even throw in the piece of land beside my meadow to show my gratitude."

Now the old man *really* couldn't resist. "I'll speak to her immediately."

And the old man did not wait. As soon as his daughter had returned home from work, he sat her down and tried to bring her to her senses.

"You *must* marry him!" he said to her after the fifth time she had refused to do just that. "He is willing to forgive the debt I owe *and* give us a piece of land. It doesn't get any better than that!"

"I won't marry him! He is a selfish old squire who only looks out for himself, and he's got terrible morals. The fact he's trying to *buy* me proves it!"

The old man was frustrated with his daughter. How could she not see what he did? "You would be doing it for *us*, my dear daughter. Just imagine what a better life we'd have with our debt paid and the extra land to grow crops or rear animals. No longer would we worry about tomorrow!"

"But it wouldn't be a good life for *me*, would it?" his daughter retorted. "For I would be married to a man I did not love!"

And so on and on they argued until the sun had set, and they became too tired to argue any further. When the young woman had gone to bed, the old man sat on a chair that had seen better days and wondered what he should do. His daughter wouldn't listen to reason, and he knew the squire would not take no for an answer.

The next morning, when the young woman had once again left for work, the squire returned.

"I'm afraid she said no," the old man told the squire.

As he had predicted, the squire did not take kindly to this news.

"That's unacceptable!" he cried. The squire stomped around the house, shouting obscenities about how the old man's daughter would be lucky to have him and how women knew absolutely nothing. Once he had calmed down, his face no longer flushed with red-hot anger, he said, "Well, the deal's off then. If she won't marry me, I won't settle your debt. In fact, I will now collect *double* interest."

The old man's life flashed before his eyes: him, paying off his debt eternally, even from the grave. No, that could not happen. He had to do something. "Ignore my daughter," he said. "The wedding will happen."

"It will?" the squire practically squealed.

"Yes. We will just have to … trick her," the old man admitted uncomfortably.

"How?"

"We will simply pretend that you have sent for her to do some work on your farm, when in fact she will be taken to the church where the vicar and wedding guests will already be waiting, and she will be so in shock that she will be swept along with no time to think it over!"

The squire agreed to the old man's suggestion, and with that they sent invitations for next week.

When the morning of the wedding came around, and the guests and the vicar were soon to be on their way to the church, the squire called for one of his farm lads' assistance.

"How can I help, sir?" the farm lad asked.

"Run down to my neighbour, will you, and

ask him to send up what he has promised me *immediately*." The squire smirked, eager for the plan to unfold. The old man would tell his daughter that she was wanted to work on the farm, and the lad would bring her along in no time! Then they could get her swiftly ready at the squire's house, and whisk her to the church.

"I can do that, sir."

"But if you are not back with her in a flash," the squire said, shaking his fist at him, "I will—" But the squire did not need to finish his sentence as the lad had run off, afraid to hear what would happen to him if he failed to deliver.

He raced down to the old man's cottage and knocked on his door.

"My master has sent me to retrieve what he asked of you, right away," the farm lad said to the old man.

"Yes, yes!" said the old man, sure the squire must have relayed the plan of trickery to the farm boy – but of course the lad knew nothing of it. "Run down to the hayfield and take her with you. Go!"

And so the lad ran off quickly and found the man's daughter merrily raking the hay.

At the sight of him, she looked up and frowned. "How can I help you?"

"Good day, miss. My master at the farm has asked me to fetch what your father has promised!"

"And what has my father promised?" the young woman asked, raising an eyebrow.

"I … I'm not sure," the farm lad answered honestly. "All I know is that it is a 'her'!"

The daughter's mind raced. She quickly understood what was happening: behind her back, her father must have agreed to give her away to the squire against her wishes. She couldn't believe he would sink to such depths! How dare he try to trick her into marriage? Well, it certainly wasn't going to happen. She was *not* going to marry the squire!

And she knew *just* how to get her revenge on both the squire and her dad…

"Ah, yes, I believe your master is talking about our little bay mare. You better go grab her!" The daughter pointed in the direction of the majestic horse with the reddish-brown coat that stood tethered not far from them.

"Great! Thank you!" said the farm lad, and he swiftly untethered the horse, jumped on her back and rode home at full speed.

When he arrived, he tethered the bay mare outside the squire's house before meeting him in the back yard.

"Have you got her with you?" the squire asked.

"Yes, sir, yes! I've left her by the door."

"That won't do! Take her up to my mother's room!" urged the squire.

The lad frowned in confusion. "But … how?"

"What do you mean 'how'? If you can't manage her alone, then get some of the other men to help you. Just do it!"

The farm lad hesitated, but upon seeing the look on the squire's face he knew there was no arguing. So he rounded up all the help he could from the other farm workers. They all thought it was a strange task indeed, but none of them wanted to question the squire. Together they took the mare into the house and up the stairs, to the room where all the wedding items fit for a bride awaited.

"That's all done then, master," the farm lad said after he returned downstairs, wiping sweat from his face, "though I must say that might have been the worst job I've ever had!"

The squire hissed at the lad. "Do not speak of

her that way. Now before I give you your silver coin, send the women up to dress her."

The farm lad's jaw dropped in shock. "But mast—"

"No arguing! She may not want what's coming but it's for the best. If she puts up a fuss, just tell them to hold her while they dress her. And oh, don't forget the wreath or crown!"

"Yes, master." The lad shook his head in disbelief before running into the kitchen where a group of ladies were waiting.

"Look, lasses," he called out, "the master has said that you are to go upstairs and dress up the bay mare – yes, the *bay mare* – as a bride." He couldn't believe he'd just uttered those words. "I think it's a joke he wants to play on the guests before the real bride comes?"

The women laughed, but did as they were asked. They struggled to get the dress over the horse's head, but managed to tug the fabric so that it draped over her shoulders and flanks. Just as the squire had instructed, they decked the mare with floral garlands and even crowned her with a beautiful wreath. When they were done, they told the lad, who in turn told the squire.

"Bring her down to the church. I will receive her at the door myself!" he said, and so the squire hurried off to the church, where the guests and the vicar were gathered.

The lad and the other farm hands brought down the bay mare with great difficulty, but they finally made it to the church, where, inside, the squire and all the guests waited with anticipation.

As the doors were flung open, the farm lad announced, "Here comes the bride!"

Everyone turned. At the sight before him, the squire's beam dropped from his face, and the guests began laughing so loudly it shook the walls of the church.

The young woman had truly made fools of the men who had tried to trick her, and she went on to live a life of her own choosing.

And the squire? Well, let's just say he didn't get married that day – and he never would either!

THREE BILLY GOATS GRUFF

In this story, three goats outwit a formidable troll to cross a bridge and reach a rich and bountiful new feeding ground. "Three Billy Goats Gruff" is a Norwegian folktale first published between 1841 and 1844 by Asbjørnsen and Moe in their Norske Folkeeventyr.

Once upon a time, there was a family of three billy goats: Papa Gruff, Big Brother Gruff and Baby Gruff. The three goats lived alone in a small valley where there once grew sweet, lush grass that could satisfy even the pickiest of eaters.

But one day, the grass on their land dried up and stopped growing. The three billy goats all stared at the ground where their favourite patch of grass had been, each of them wondering what they could do next. They had to eat – they were always very hungry after all – but how could they have their fill when there was hardly anything left?

"Why don't we plant more grass?" Baby Gruff asked. Baby Gruff was the littlest of them all, not even half the size of his brother, and his horns had barely begun to grow. "I'm sure I can find a way!"

"It's not that easy, my son," Papa Gruff responded with a sad smile. "The land is dying. Even if we try, it will not grow."

Baby Gruff thought again. He was a dreamer who always looked on the bright side. "Why don't we eat something else instead?" he suggested. "There are still some trees. We could nibble their branches."

"For a short time, perhaps," sighed Papa Gruff. "But we need grass if we are going to thrive."

"I know what we could do," Big Brother Gruff said. He was tired this morning, as he most often was. These days, he was staying up well past his bedtime to explore the surrounding land in the quiet of the night, discovering what there was to see beyond their valley. "We can always cross the bridge."

Papa Gruff let out a bleat in panic. "You cannot be serious, son!"

"Oh, but I am." Big Brother Gruff stomped on the ground. "There's more than enough grass on the other side of the bridge – I've seen it. From the top of the hill, all you can see is the tall green grass on the other side."

"When have you seen this?" Papa Gruff asked, certain he had not allowed his son to go any further than their marked area.

"When you've all been asleep, I've been investigating," Big Brother Gruff said proudly. "I thought the day might come when we ran out of grass."

Papa Gruff's mouth hung open, his beard nearly touching the ground. "But son, there is a *troll* under that bridge. We couldn't possibly cross."

The three billy goats were all too aware of the

troll that lived there, eagerly waiting to eat anybody who dared to cross his bridge. That was, after all, how Mama Gruff had died.

"No, I simply will not allow it!" Papa Gruff cried. "We are not losing anybody else to that troll."

"So instead we starve?" Big Brother Gruff argued. "Papa, what else is there to do? We cannot live much longer if we stay here."

Papa Gruff knew his son was right, but he did not dare cross that bridge. So many goats from their herd over the years had been lost to that troll. Mama Gruff had been strong, but even she had not managed to cross that bridge without being devoured. The mere thought of that fateful day caused a shiver to run through his body. No, he would not allow his children to cross that bridge. They would have to think of some other way to find food.

The three goats slowly ate the grass they had left, only allowing themselves small portions to save just enough for another day. As they grazed, they pondered what to do once the last of the grass had gone.

Suddenly, Baby Gruff squealed, struck by an idea. "We can trick the troll!" he said, his eyes flashing.

Papa Gruff's interest was piqued. "Trick him how?"

"Oh, here we go again. Another one of your ideas." Big Brother Gruff rolled his eyes at his little brother, but even so he was curious to hear what Baby Gruff had to say. "Go on then. Don't leave us hanging – we don't have much longer left!"

And so Baby Gruff told them his idea, bursting with excitement at his plan to get past the troll without sacrificing any of their lives. Big Brother Gruff and Papa Gruff both listened to the littlest Gruff patiently.

"I think … that might actually work," Big Brother Gruff admitted when Baby Gruff was finished, surprising not only himself but also everyone else – so much so that Baby Gruff fell over on his side in joy!

"I did it! I helped!" Baby Gruff bleated.

"Papa, what do you think?" Big Brother Gruff asked.

It was a good idea. An *excellent* idea, in fact. But did he dare go through with it? So many had been slain by the troll. Could they really be the first ones to cross the bridge safely? There was so much at risk, in particular to Papa Gruff, if they were to go along with Baby Gruff's plan. But Papa Gruff couldn't help but think of the single solemn patch of grass left, only enough to feed one of them tonight. Although he would give up his share for his children in a heartbeat, he knew it also meant he would have to decide which one of his children deserved more.

Either they remained here in the valley and starved to death, or they attempted to cross the bridge, risking the same fate as Mama Gruff. They could die either way, but Baby Gruff's idea had a slim chance of success. It seemed that going along with it was the only option.

"Fine," Papa Gruff said finally, and his children let out an audible breath. He was surprised to notice that they weren't as frightened as he was. It surely was a sign that they had a piece of their mother within them: her courage. "Let's face that troll once and for all."

And so they began on their journey to cross the bridge. But not together – no, that would not do. Instead, Baby Gruff went on ahead, while Big Brother Gruff and Papa Gruff watched from afar, hiding behind a large rock.

Baby Gruff, despite his size, was the bravest of

them all. He didn't even look back as his hooves trod heavily and noisily across the wooden bridge, shaking the rickety boards. In his eagerness to cross the bridge, he had momentarily forgotten that the plan was to do so *quietly*.

Suddenly, a roar came from beneath the bridge, causing the boards to shake even more. Papa Gruff watched from afar as Baby Gruff wobbled, his legs aching to stomp over there and take care of his kid. But he couldn't. If he did, the plan would be forsaken, and Baby Gruff's efforts would have been for nothing. Meanwhile, Big Brother Gruff shielded his eyes behind the rock.

"Who dares trip-trapping over my bridge?" the troll bellowed before rearing into view.

Baby Gruff nearly fell over again, this time not out of excitement but from fear. The troll was ten times his size and smelled more horrible than you could ever imagine. He was as green as the sweet grass that the goats once nibbled upon, but all along his body were bumps of grey and brown, almost like he was covered in rocks. He wore a tattered vest and shorts that were too small for him, and brandished a wooden bat with spikes all over it. It was safe to say that Baby Gruff was scared with a capital 'S'.

"I ... I'm Baby Gruff," he responded to the troll. "I am just going to cross your brid—"

"Nobody crosses my bridge!" The troll's words boomed out of his mouth and caused the littlest Gruff to stumble backwards. "If they try, I eat them!"

"Well..." Baby Gruff held his head up high, trying to exude confidence in his words. "You wouldn't want to eat *me*."

"And why would that be?"

"Because I'm too little. Just look at me! I'm hardly the size of your bat!"

The troll inspected his bat before nodding in confirmation. "That is true. Even so, I can eat you as a snack. Now if you will just be quiet..."

Baby Gruff knew he was almost out of time. As much as it pained him to do so, he said, "If you wait until I have passed, you can have my brother. He's right behind me and he is *so* much bigger than I am. Practically twice the size! Imagine what a feast that would be!"

"Why can't I just have the both of you? You can be my starter and he can be my main."

"But my brother will only cross this bridge if I make it to the other side *safely*. That means I cannot be eaten."

The troll considered the littlest Gruff and, after what felt like an eternity, said, "Well, be off with you then. I'll wait for your juicy brother to come stomping along."

The troll returned to his hiding place under the bridge. Baby Gruff dashed across the bridge before the troll could change his mind. When he got to the other side, he could hardly believe he had made it.

Now there was only his brother and his father left. To signal that he had made it to the other side, he let out a loud bleat.

"It worked," Papa Gruff said in awe. "He made it across the bridge. Baby Gruff managed to cross the bridge unharmed."

"Guess it's my turn." Big Brother Gruff got up from behind the rock and looked ahead at the bridge, his brother safely on the other side.

Big Brother Gruff was not convinced he would enjoy the same fate. Baby Gruff's plan to trick the troll into thinking that there was a bigger and better feast coming his way shortly was good, but what were the chances he would fall for it again? Big Brother Gruff, unlike his brother, was a realist.

Big Brother Gruff trod slowly towards the bridge,

the *trip-trap* of his steps on the wood loud enough to numb his own ears.

"Who's that trip-trapping over my bridge?" the troll shouted, and he rose once again from his hiding place.

Big Brother Gruff couldn't help but recoil in disgust at the troll's bulbous, warty nose and his reeking breath, which smelled like a cross between wet straw and sewage sludge. The billy goat was especially disgusted by the troll's smile, which showcased several huge, uneven teeth that must have chomped on who knew how many of Big Brother Gruff's departed friends. "Well, if it isn't my next meal!"

"Look, I'm going to level with you." Big Brother Gruff sighed. "I know my brother said you'd get to eat me if you let him cross the bridge, but the truth is, you won't."

"No?" the troll scoffed at Big Brother Gruff. How dare the goat defy him? "And why is that?"

"Because behind me is my father, and he is even bigger than me and would make for an excellent feast. But he will only cross the bridge if I reach the other side safely."

"I've heard this before, and yet you came here

telling me it was a lie. You goats won't fool me again!"

The troll neared Big Brother Gruff, but even so the goat didn't move.

"I'm not fooling you. I promise you that my father is much bigger and much tastier. He's as old as you are, if not older, and has aged like fine wine. I guarantee you, he will make a scrumptious meal!"

"And you promise that after you there is only your father left to cross the bridge?"

"I promise." And Big Brother Gruff told the truth. After his father, there were no goats left in the valley.

"Very well, be off with you then!" said the troll after careful consideration.

This time, the troll did not go back to his hiding place. Instead, he hovered by the bridge, awaiting his next meal.

Big Brother Gruff dashed across the bridge. To signal to Papa Gruff that it was time, he let out the longest bleat he could muster before tucking into the sweet grass next to Baby Gruff.

"I told you it would work," Baby Gruff said in between bites.

"Yeah, yeah. Let's just hope Dad's able to pull off his part," Big Brother Gruff said.

Just then, Papa Gruff boldly placed his hooves on the bridge, trip-trapping with as much force as he could, channelling his wife's courage and power as he prepared for the final step of their plan.

"Well then, who is this trip-trapping over my bridge?" the troll asked.

"It is I, the biggest billy goat of them all. I've come to join my children on the other side of the bridge."

"Oh no, you haven't," the troll said defiantly, brandishing his bat. "Your children have promised me a scrumptious meal, and I will wait no longer to claim it."

"I don't think my children have promised you anything. I think that's just your greed talking."

"How dare you speak back to me!" The troll bared his sharp, wonky teeth at Papa Gruff. "Enough talking. It's time to eat!"

The troll rushed towards Papa Gruff, and for a brief second of ice-cold fear, the goat thought he couldn't go ahead with the plan after all. But then he summoned up all the love he had for his children and his late wife, and Papa Gruff charged ahead at the troll, bleating out, "This one's for my family!"

As the two came head to head, Papa Gruff caught

the troll with his spear-like horns, causing the creature to yelp in pain. With all his strength, Papa Gruff used those strong horns to toss the weakened troll into the rapid stream below – and soon his body was carried away, further and further from his home.

With the troll long gone, Papa Gruff trotted over to his boys. The family of goats huddled up, bleating with joy.

"You were so brave, Papa!" cried Baby Gruff.

"Ah, you were the brave one, crossing that bridge first." Papa Gruff smiled.

"The plan worked! We did it!" Baby Gruff exclaimed.

Big Brother Gruff rolled his eyes at his brother, but even he couldn't hold back the pride he felt in Baby Gruff. "We sure did."

"And now," Papa Gruff said, looking up at the sky as if his wife were listening to him, "we will eat all this grass, parade around all the rich fields of this valley and live happily ever after."

THE TWELVE WILD DUCKS

This tale is about a queen who has twelve sons but desperately desires a daughter and so strikes a deal with a witch – but if she wants a daughter, she must give up her sons... There are many similarities between this story and "Snow White", since it is based on a similar folktale structure.

Once upon a time, lived a queen with twelve sons but no daughters.

One day in winter, when she was out driving in the freshly fallen snow, her nose began to bleed. She stopped her horses and left the carriage, picked up some of the white snow and placed it against her nose to help stop the bleeding. As she leaned against a fence, she couldn't help but think about how long she had wished for a daughter. "If only I had a little girl to call my own, with skin as white as snow and lips as red as blood…"

Just then, an old witch came up to her and asked, "Did I hear that you want a daughter?"

"Yes, that is correct," the queen sniffled. "I tried to have one for years, but all I've got are sons. Not that I don't love them … I just always wished I could have a daughter. My sons … they all take after their father in every way, and we have so little in common. I just wish one of my children were more like me!"

The witch narrowed her eyes. "How *much* do you want a daughter?" she asked.

"Oh, more than anything in this world!" cried the queen.

"Well, if it is a daughter you want, then it is a

daughter you will have," said the witch. "But only for the price of your sons."

The queen gasped. "You cannot have my sons!"

"Oh, but do you not want a daughter more than anything in this world?"

The queen hesitated. She wanted a daughter *so* badly. It was all she had ever dreamed of. But her sons…

"Let's make this easier for you," the witch said. "I will give you a daughter and allow you to keep all of your sons until she is christened."

The queen was torn. She did not want to give up her sons, but she was desperate for a daughter. She decided to agree, convinced she could hide her daughter's christening from the witch so she would never be forced to complete the bargain.

Nine months later, the queen had a daughter, just like the witch had promised. The little girl had skin as white as snow and lips as red as blood. They aptly called her Snow-White and Rose-Red, though for short they called her Rosie.

The queen could hardly believe it: she finally had the little girl she had always dreamed of.

But the queen's joy did not last long. She tried her best to keep the news of Rosie's birth quiet and invited nobody but her close family to the child's christening. But as Rosie was baptized, the queen spotted the old witch lurking at the back of the church with a wicked smile on her face.

The queen gasped and held on to her daughter tightly.

"What are you doing here?" the queen demanded.

"Oh, I am here to collect what I am owed. Or have you forgotten the bargain that you made?"

The queen swallowed the lump in her throat. "You cannot be serious."

"Oh, but I am. You promised to give up your sons, and so you shall." Then the old witch chanted a spell and snapped her fingers.

Suddenly, the twelve princes transformed into wild ducks! Before the queen could cry out for them, the ducks flapped their wings and flew out of the church.

"My sons!" The queen raced outside, only to find her sons high and distant in the sky. "Come back!"

But come back they did not.

From that day onwards, the queen mourned her sons but focused all her love and attention on her daughter, who grew up healthy and beautiful. But despite a lifestyle suitable for a princess, Rosie was always sorrowful and nobody could understand why.

For a long time, she could not put it into words. But one evening, the princess finally explained to the queen what caused her so much pain.

"I'm lonely," she said simply. "Everybody else has siblings, but I don't. I just … feel alone."

The queen's lip quivered. For so long they had shielded Rosie from the truth. She had not been able to bear telling Rosie that she, too, had brothers, but perhaps now was the time.

"You had siblings," the queen said.

"I did?" said Rosie.

"Yes." The queen sighed. "I had twelve sons before you, but I gave them all up in exchange for you." The queen recounted the story of the old witch, her mistaken hope that the bargain would not come to pass, and how her sons had turned into wild ducks.

"I didn't think she would actually stick to her word, but even despite how terrible it was, how can I regret my actions? Without them, I would not have you. I would have done anything to have you." The queen wept. "All I ever wanted was a daughter!"

Rosie did not know how to react. It was because

of *her* that the castle was so quiet and that she felt so lonely! If she had not existed, there would be so much liveliness, laughter and love in this home. Now there was nothing but her mother's weeping.

"I must go and search for them." Rosie stood up. "I'll find them and I'll break the curse somehow, so that we can all be reunited again!"

"No, you can't!" The queen leaped up and grabbed her daughter's wrists. "I can't lose you, too – please!"

Despite her mother's desperation, the princess would not back down. "I need to do this. I will never feel happy again unless I can be reunited with my brothers and make things right."

The queen wept as her daughter left the castle without even a glance over her shoulder.

Rosie walked and walked, travelling for weeks on end, through all manner of weather, until she finally came to a little hut on a worn forest path.

"Hello?" she called out as she entered the cabin. "Is anybody here?"

No response came, but Rosie's heart lifted at the sight of twelve of everything: twelve beds, bowls, chairs and so much more. Her brother's *had* to be here! After she lit a fire to warm herself up, she heard the flapping of wings. When she turned around, she saw a dozen birds flying towards the hut, and when they crossed the threshold, they turned into young men.

"It's mighty toasty in here!" said the youngest prince before his eyes landed on Rosie. "Wait, who are you?"

Rosie threw her arms around several of her brothers in turn, responding, "I am your sister! I've been walking for weeks to find you!"

The princes looked at one another in surprise. Unlike their sister, they weren't too pleased to be reunited.

Removing himself from her grasp, the eldest prince asked, "Why? So you could gloat about how *you're* the one living in Mother and Father's castle as a human while we spend our days as ducks and outcasts?"

The venom in her brother's voice was unmistakable, but Rosie had known that this was not going to be easy. It was because of her after all that they were in this situation.

"I am here to save you, not to gloat. I'll do anything to break this curse and free you, if you just tell me how," she said.

The eldest brother could hear the sincerity in his sister's voice and softened. "There is one way you could help but it will be difficult," he admitted.

"I told you," Rosie said with determination, "I will do *anything* to free you."

"The witch told us of one way the curse can be broken. You need to gather cotton grass, and once collected you will need to card it, spin it and weave it into cloth. From the cloth you then need to cut and sew twelve shirts, one for each brother," the eldest explained.

Rosie nodded. "I will do it," she said.

"I haven't reached the most important part," her brother warned. "You need to do all this without once talking, laughing or crying. If you can do that, then we will be set free once and for all."

The princess closed her eyes. It would be difficult, but she could do it. She had to. "Just tell me, where can I find enough cotton grass for so many shirts?"

Her brother looked down at his feet. "Unfortunately, you can only get the cotton grass from the witches' moor."

"Then I'll do just that. Trust me, my brothers, I will succeed," Rosie declared.

And so the princess headed to the witches' moor.

The warm sun watched over her as she plucked at the great crop of cotton grass.

She returned home to the hut a few hours later with as much cotton grass as she could carry. She carded it, but when she spun it into yarn, she realized she hadn't plucked nearly enough for twelve shirts. But night was falling, and she was afraid that if she returned to the moor now she would run into the witches who would undoubtedly be up to no good.

So she went back to the moor the following morning. As she was plucking the cotton grass again, a young king was out hunting. He was so struck by Rosie's beauty that he stopped by the door when he saw her, hoping she might wish to speak with him.

"Who are you, my fair lady?" he asked.

Of course, Rosie was forbidden to speak while she tried to break the curse, so he received no answer. She simply smiled warmly.

"Hmm, are you a little shy?" he asked.

Rosie shook her head, her eyes sparkling.

"Playing hard to get, perhaps?" he teased, and the princess had to try hard to hold in a laugh.

The young king was intrigued by Rosie's

mysterious silence and the delicate way she plucked the cotton grass.

"Would you like to take a rest and come for tea at my castle?" he offered.

Rosie would have liked to accompany the king, but she wrung her hands and pointed to the full sacks of cotton grass.

"Ah, you must keep working?" he said.

Rosie nodded.

"Then I will stay and help you until the job is complete," the king offered.

Despite being unable to use her voice, Rosie found the young king to be agreeable. She admired his good humour and kindness in helping her gather the cotton grass.

When late evening came, the young king motioned towards his horse.

"I'd say we are done now, wouldn't you? We've got so many sacks!"

Rosie nodded.

"Well, why don't you come visit my castle? I would love to have you," he offered, and Rosie agreed nodding gladly. With the bags tied to the horse, they rode off to the king's castle.

But when they arrived, the young king's

stepmother laid eyes on Rosie's snow-white skin and blood-red lips and was filled with jealousy, anger and suspicion.

After they had all had tea together, the stepmother pulled the king aside and said, "Why have you brought her home? You tried to make conversation, and yet she doesn't speak. You told many jokes, and yet she doesn't laugh. You told the sad tale of your mother's death, and yet she doesn't cry! Don't you see that those are telltale signs of a witch?"

The young king brushed off his stepmother's concerns. "Nonsense, stepmother. She is wonderful, and I am intent on marrying her."

Rosie had overheard the conversation and could not help but be pleased by the young king's reaction. He could have very well agreed with his stepmother; it *was* strange after all that she didn't say anything! So when the young king asked her to marry him, she was delighted to nod in agreement.

They married soon after and lived together at the king's castle, but the princess – now queen – had not forgotten her promise to her brothers. She spent her nights spinning cotton grass and sewing shirts.

Many weeks had passed, and Rosie had made good progress on her shirts, but as she reached the twelfth and final shirt, she realized that she had not collected enough cotton grass to complete it. Even though she was afraid to run into the witches, she knew she had no choice but to leave straight away. Grabbing her cloak, she slipped out of the palace at midnight and went to pick some more.

Now all would have been well if it hadn't been for her husband's stepmother, who saw her leave and was certain that she was up to no good ... perhaps because she herself was up to no good. For she was in fact the witch who turned Rosie's brothers into ducks!

The stepmother hurried to her stepson's chamber and awoke him.

"Your bride is up to no good! I've just seen with my own eyes that she has gone to the witches' moor! Now why would she do that unless she was meeting up with other wicked company?"

"You're talking rubbish," he said with tired eyes.

"No, come see for yourself!" she insisted.

The king reluctantly agreed and went with his stepmother to the edge of the moor. He could not believe his eyes but right there, underneath the moonlight, stood his bride next to the witches. He gasped audibly.

"Can you see it now?" his stepmother whispered. "She is a *witch*! And we cannot have a queen who is a witch! We must burn her at the stake!"

The king turned away from his bride, torn between his love for her and what he had seen with his own eyes. In the end, he reluctantly agreed with his stepmother. It was the laws of the land after all that witchcraft was not to be tolerated – even if practised by the love of your life.

The next day, piles of wood were gathered on the court square, and the stepmother herself set it ablaze. The king's men pulled the queen from her bedchamber, telling her she had been discovered to be a witch and must suffer the consequences.

Rosie was horrified but thought quickly – she had to save her brothers, even if it was the last thing she did. She gestured desperately for the king's men to take the twelve shirts she had made and lay them on twelve boards around the fire. All of the shirts were complete except for the one for her youngest brother, which was still missing a sleeve.

The men had hardly finished doing as the queen had ordered before twelve ducks swooped down from the sky and snatched away the shirts.

"That has to be witchcraft," the stepmother told

anybody who would listen. "Quick, we must burn her immediately before she does anything else!"

But the very next moment, twelve young men came riding into the courtyard, each one dressed as a prince, except for the youngest who had a duck's wing instead of a left arm.

"What's going on here?" demanded the eldest prince.

"Sadly, my queen is to be burned as she has proved to be a witch," said the king.

"That's not true," said the youngest prince. "Sister, you can speak now! You've saved us!"

Rosie was hesitant. She didn't feel as if she had saved them. Her youngest brother still had a wing for an arm.

"Speak. I'd rather have a wing for an arm than not have a sister any more," the youngest said as he read the hesitation in her eyes.

And so Rosie did, recounting the story of what she had promised to do to save her brothers from the horrid curse that had been put on them. The king and his people were engrossed as they listened to the tale. Only the wicked stepmother trembled with fear.

"Quench the fire! My wife is not to be burned!" the king proclaimed.

"Well, somebody needs to be burned," the eldest prince said, "for my sister would not even be in this situation had it not been for *her*!"

Everyone turned to see who the prince pointed at and were shocked to find that it was the stepmother.

"Me? You must be mistaken," the stepmother laughed.

"No, I am not. You see, my brothers and I have flown far and wide and we have spoken to many who can attest that *you* are the witch who placed the curse on us!" cried one of the princes.

The king looked at his stepmother with anger. "How could you do that? And how could you try to trick me into harming my own wife?"

The stepmother scrambled for words. "Please … I raised you. Have mercy."

"I will spare your life. But you are to be banished from this land for ever!" the king called out. "Take her away!"

The stepmother bowed her head in defeat. She was taken away, and the king turned to his wife.

"I am so sorry that I believed her lies," he said to his wife. "I shouldn't have."

"No, you shouldn't have," she said, her voice

slightly raspy from not using it for so long. "But now you know why I have been silent for so long."

The king smiled at his wife, falling in love with her all over again at the melody of her voice.

"Let's go home. And bring your brothers, too. We have a lot to celebrate."

Rosie smiled and reached her hand out to her brothers. "Yes. And we must invite my mother. She will be so pleased to see her family reunited at last."

WHY THE SEA IS SALTY

This tale has many versions and is widely told around Europe, but there are also stories from as far as the Philippines that try to explain why the sea is salty. This is just one of many of them, with a message about being grateful for what you have.

Once upon a time, there were two brothers: one elder brother, who was very rich but unkind, and a younger brother, who was poor yet generous.

On the day before Christmas Eve, the poor brother found that he and his wife had not a bite to eat in their house or any money to buy food. They'd even looked around their house for items they could spare to sell but found nothing.

"Oh, my love," the poor brother's wife cried. "What are we going to do?"

"I'm not sure," her husband answered, for he simply did not know. Well, he knew *one* thing he could do. He just didn't want to do it.

"Why don't you ask your brother?" his wife suggested. "Surely he can spare us something for Christmas Eve?"

The poor man wasn't fond of his brother, for he was selfish, but what else could he do? His wife was in tears, and the last thing he wanted was to disappoint her.

So he put on a cloak that had seen better days and went to visit his brother.

"Please, brother," he said when he reached the rich man's door. "We have absolutely nothing. I beg of you to help us out so we may have something to eat."

The rich brother paused before he spoke. "I will give you a cut of beef. But only if you do one thing for me."

"Whatever it is, I'll do it!" the poor brother vowed.

"Here is the cut of beef – now go to Hel," the rich brother said before shoving a steak into his brother's hands.

The poor brother's mouth watered at the sight of the steak, and he couldn't think straight. "Thank you, brother! You have no idea how you have saved us!"

As the poor brother walked home with the steak tucked in his cloak, he thought about his rich brother's words and realized that this beef must not be for himself and his wife to eat after all. Instead, he had been sent on an errand. The steak was for a man named Hel, and he knew that as hungry as he was, a promise was a promise.

He spent hours traipsing through the forest to find the man named Hel, determined not to break his word. Along the way he met an old man with a long beard chopping Yule logs.

"Excuse me, I am looking for Hel. Could you tell me, am I on the right track?" the poor man asked.

The old man nodded. "Keep walking straight and soon enough you will get to Hel. Though be cautious: I see you have steak with you. Hel *loves* beef and he will do anything to get it from you. Whatever you do, do *not*, I repeat, do *not* accept any of his offers."

The poor man was surprised. He had been planning to simply hand the steak over to Hel free of charge. But what if his brother never gave him any food of his own? Perhaps this was an opportunity for him to earn something for himself and his wife at last.

"Then what *should* I do?" he asked.

"Ask him for his millstone. Even if he refuses at first, stay firm that it is the only item you will trade the beef steak for. Trust me, it will be worth it. With the magic of the millstone, you will never be poor again," said the old man.

"Thank you for your help," the poor man said before walking on.

In only a matter of minutes he came across Hel's door. He rapped on it, and as he was let in, he found that, just as the old man had warned, Hel's eyes lit up at the sight of the steak in his hands.

"What have we here?" said Hel. "Is that for me?

I certainly hope it is, for I haven't tasted meat in nearly five decades!"

Hel lunged at the poor man, swiping at the steak, but the poor man was prepared and held it at arm's length from him. "You can only have this cut of beef if I can have your millstone."

Hel was taken aback by the poor man's request. "How about some coins instead?"

"No, the millstone is what I want." The poor man stood his ground.

"What about some clothes instead?" said Hel. "Your cloak looks like it's seen better days."

"No, the millstone, please."

Hel sighed. "What about precious gems? I have all kinds!"

"Again, all I want is the millstone," the poor man insisted.

Hel bit his nails. He hadn't eaten meat in so long but he did not want to give up the millstone either. In the end, he couldn't contain his hunger and gave in. "Fine! You can have the millstone. But do you even know how to use it?"

"No … I was hoping you would tell me how to use it."

Hel shook his head. Why had this man asked

for something he had no inkling of how to use? He begrudgingly explained. "Whatever you wish for, just say, 'Grind, my millstone!' Once you have enough of whatever it is you wish for, then say, 'Enough and done!' and it will stop."

The poor man's eyes widened. "Truly? And it's that simple?" It seemed too easy.

"It's that simple. Now go!"

The poor man wrapped the magic millstone in his cloak and walked until he reached his home.

When he arrived, his wife was an utter mess.

"Where have you been all this time?" she cried. "I thought you had gone missing or were dead!"

"I promise, I have a good explanation," said the poor man, and so he told his wife the tale of how he had retrieved the millstone from Hel. "Now let's try it out." He rubbed his hands together for warmth. "Grind, my millstone! We would like a feast!"

The millstone began to grind, and before their eyes appeared meat, beer and so much pudding you could nearly drown in it! It truly was a feast for royalty. The poor man and woman ate until there was no more room in their stomachs.

"Enough and done!" the poor man commanded, remembering what Hel had taught him earlier.

The millstone had ground enough food for a few days, but they realized that food was not the only item they had been lacking recently: their clothes were so torn and raggedy they were not even fit to be repurposed.

"Grind, my millstone! We would like some new clothes!"

As before, the magic millstone began to grind, and it did not take long before the couple had new fine clothes to wear.

"Enough and done!" the poor man said when there were enough clothes to last them a lifetime.

From that day on, they never lacked anything ever again. The millstone did as instructed, giving them a new house, soil that could grow crops, and so much more. In fact, they soon had so much that they hardly needed to use the millstone any more.

When the rich brother got wind of his younger brother's change of fortune, he was horribly irritated. One day, his brother had been at his door begging for a slab of meat and now he had so much he was giving it away to people as if he were a king!

Annoyed and envious, the older brother marched up to his younger brother's door and demanded, "How did you become so rich?!"

"It's funny, actually," the poor brother said. "You helped me!"

"I did?"

"Yes. Remember when I came to you asking for some food for Christmas Eve? You told me to take the cut of beef and go to Hel. Well, I did exactly that. And when I delivered the meat to him, Hel gave me a magic millstone in exchange."

The rich brother's jaw dropped. He could not believe that he had unintentionally had a hand in his brother's good fortune! "Well, show me this millstone. I must see how this machine has helped you receive your good fortune."

The poor brother put the millstone on the table and called, "Grind, my millstone! We would like good food to eat!"

The millstone began to grind and quickly poured out delicious meals for the two brothers: loaves of bread, buttered potatoes and slabs of top-quality meat.

The rich brother's mouth watered as he stared in disbelief. He may already have been rich, but he was greedy. He *needed* that millstone.

"Sell it to me," he demanded of his younger brother.

The poor brother was shocked. "It's not for sale."

"Well, lend it to me then!" The older brother rolled his eyes. "If it weren't for me, you wouldn't have it in the first place."

This at least was true. He did owe his brother for sending him on the journey to Hel, didn't he?

"You can only have it for one day, OK?" the poor brother offered.

"Fine, whatever, I'll take it!" The rich brother snatched the millstone out of his younger brother's hands and practically ran off with it, before his brother even had a chance to explain how it worked.

The rich brother knew exactly what he would do with the millstone: he would have it grind out salt for the fishermen who were salting their fish. It would make their jobs easier, and the rich brother could sell his service for a fortune! He ran to his boat and rowed out to sea.

He pulled out the millstone and laid it on the boat. "Grind, my millstone! Give me *saaaaalt*!"

The millstone began to grind again, pouring out the finest grains of salt imaginable. It poured so much that the boat was soon full.

When the brother was satisfied, he asked it to stop. "Now stop, my millstone!"

But nothing happened.

"I said, stop grinding! I have enough salt!"

Still, the millstone kept turning.

"What is happening? Why is it still going?" he asked himself, beginning to panic. "I said, *stop*!"

The millstone kept grinding and pouring out salt despite the man's desperate pleading.

"Perhaps if I throw it in the sea, it will simply stop," he said.

And so he tried to throw the millstone overboard, but he could not lift it! It was far heavier now than it had been before, laden with all this salt. He could not for the life of him understand what was happening.

Soon the boat was so full of salt that it began to sink.

"Help! I need help!" the man cried, but there was nobody close enough to hear him.

It didn't take long before the boat, along with the man and the millstone, sank to the bottom of the sea. The greedy man was never seen again.

And the magic millstone?

It never stopped turning. Each passing day, it is said to continue grinding out the finest salt, filling the whole ocean.

THE FOX CHEATS THE BEAR OUT OF HIS CHRISTMAS FARE

This is an amusing tale about a fox and a bear who promise not to eat a special stick of butter until Christmas Eve. The fox, however, has different ideas... The story was originally published in Rinhelihorn and Other Tales from Northern Norway, *which was divided into two volumes between 1925 and 1926.*

Once upon a time, in the depths of Bøkeskogen – the Beech Tree Forest – lived a fox and a bear. For years the pair had lived together in their quaint little log cabin nestled between the trees, overlooking a pond where the occasional ducks would make a kerfuffle. If you were to approach their home, you'd be surprised to find the door slightly ajar, inviting in anybody who happened to be passing by.

The cabin itself was simple but cosy, with a roaring fireplace that kept the inhabitants warm throughout the winter. There were shelves of books that the fox would read and collections of jars that the bear had "borrowed" from people who had gone camping throughout the summer. And, in the middle of the cabin, there were two beds – a child-sized bed for the fox and a queen-sized one for the bear – in which the two rested after a long day of fooling one another.

Because make no mistake: *that* is what the fox and the bear did. If you thought that after years of trickery they would have tired themselves out, you would be very wrong indeed. And this day was no different…

"Bear!" the fox shouted as soon as his eyes opened.

"Fox?" the bear grumbled, his eyes still shut despite the light shining through the windows.

"Get up! We must go to the market! We haven't got our food for Christmas Eve dinner, which is in *two* nights, and we are running out of time!"

The bear, although tired, could not help but sit up straight and rub his eyes. "But I thought you went shopping yesterday?"

"Well, I *did*. It's just..."

"What?"

The fox looked at the bear with shame on his face. "I might have got hungry in the night and eaten it all..."

The bear sighed. This was not the first time the fox had emptied out their cupboards. "Oh, Fox, what shall I do with you?"

"Feed me?" the fox suggested with a glint in his eye.

The bear laughed. "Come on then. Let's go to the market."

At the market, the pair perused the stalls, but found nothing left but potatoes. All that they had expected to see – duck, turkey, carrots, parsnips and so much more – had already been bought!

"Oh, what's that?" the fox asked, pointing

somewhere behind the bear as they passed by a stall.

"Only the finest butter in the county," a salesperson told them. "This is imported straight from Finland. It's dense, velvety and the glossy sheen is enough to make your mouth water. Oh, why don't the two of you try a sample?"

The salesperson grabbed two small teaspoons of butter and handed it to the pair. Upon first taste, the two closed their eyes with pleasure. The butter was just salty enough, with so many flavours, and it smelled almost floral.

"Bear, we must have it!" the fox said.

The bear did not disagree. The butter they had tasted *was* the finest of them all. But he hesitated. "Should we not wait until Christmas Eve? I fear with your stomach that it won't last until then!"

"Oh, but my friends," the salesperson interjected, "I am leaving the stall after today. I am travelling east and won't be back again until next year. Either you buy it now or miss out..."

"Bear!" The fox tugged at the bear's arm. "You heard him. We *must* buy it now or we won't have it this Christmas. And we must! We just have to!"

The bear sighed. Again, he agreed. But he was so

worried the delicacy wouldn't last until Christmas with the fox's appetite!

"Only if you promise me you won't even *think* about going near the butter until Christmas Eve. OK?" The bear was stern. He was already planning to use it to roast their potatoes to perfection for Christmas Eve dinner.

"I promise, I promise!"

And so they bought the stick of butter, but it did not go in the larder along with their other food. The bear decided they needed to hide it where it would not easily tempt them. After storing away their other groceries, they hid the butter under a thick tree a distance away from their cabin.

Once they had returned home, they were both tired from their excursion.

"Midday nap?" proposed the fox.

"Midday nap," the bear agreed.

When they had both lain for some time, and the bear had begun to snore, the fox felt a temptation he could not resist.

Cautiously he crept out of his bed, ensuring that the floorboards did not creak under his weight. Then he muffled a squeal of excitement before sneaking out of the house towards the hidden stick of butter.

He promised himself he would only take the smallest of nibbles from the butter, but before he knew it a third of it was already gone! Quickly, he put the butter back where it had been hidden and rushed back to the cabin, where the bear was now awake.

"Oh, there you are. I was worrying about you," the bear said as the fox came in, out of breath from his run.

"No need! All is well!"

"Well, where you have been? And why is your mouth so greasy?"

The fox felt his heart beat louder as he tried to think of a lie. "Oh, this? This isn't grease. This is … water."

"Water?"

"Yes. Can you believe that I was asked to attend a baptism and wet the baby's head myself?" The fox laughed, but even he knew his story didn't sound real.

"Really? That's odd. What was the child called?"

"Er…" The fox couldn't think of a single name and blurted out his first thought. "Tellan Fibbs. First name Tellan. Last name Fibbs."

The bear considered the fox for a moment, his brows furrowing in confusion. "What a strange name. But, oh well, come now. Let's sleep again. I am tired still and you must be, too. Especially after the afternoon you've had."

But the fox could not stay asleep for long because his mind was buzzing with the idea of taking another bite of the delicious butter. He tried to resist but whenever he shut his eyes, all he could see was the golden brick that made his tastebuds tingle.

"Just one more time," he whispered to himself before escaping once again. This time, he ate more than a third before he put it back and returned to the cabin.

"Where have you been now?" the bear asked, no longer asleep. "Really, Fox, you must start leaving notes."

"Yes, sorry, Bear. I will do so in future." The fox tried to get past the bear to the larder, hoping the conversation was over, but the bear was not letting go.

"Well?" the bear asked.

"Well, what?"

"Well, where you have been, Fox?"

"Oh. Yes. I was … actually, can you believe that I was asked to perform *another* baptism? I must really have impressed people the first time."

"Hmm. And what was this baby's name?"

The fox looked around for inspiration before landing on the clock hanging above their stove. "Justin Thyme."

The bear would have thought more about the fox's response, but he was tired from his interrupted sleep, and worrying about where the fox had been wasn't helping. "These humans are odd creatures. Now come. No more ceremonies for you. I am absolutely exhausted."

The fox said he was not, under *any* circumstance, going to perform another baptism.

But eating the butter, on the other hand…

It took only a few minutes before the bear was snoring again. In a flash, the fox had scurried off to the hiding place and eaten what remained of the stick of butter!

Fortunately, when he returned to the cabin this time, the bear was fast asleep and was not able to question him. Now with his belly full and his tastebuds satisfied, the fox, too, fell asleep.

The next day, the bear insisted they visit

the butter to ensure it had not been discovered overnight. But when they got there, of course, it was gone!

"Who took it?" the bear growled.

"I don't know," the fox said, pretending to be shocked and distressed over the missing butter. "Maybe it was one of the hares!"

But this time the bear did not fall for the fox's lie. "It was *you*, wasn't it? Admit it!"

"No, it wasn't! Tell me, when would I have found the time?"

"Well, when you've been going to those christenings of yours! Who goes to so many ceremonies in one day?"

The fox gulped. "Bear, I told you, the babies … they needed me."

The bear harrumphed.

"Actually, Bear, while I was out christening the children … who is to say that *you* didn't go and eat the butter?"

The bear was filled with shock. "How could you accuse me of such a thing? I am not the one with a voracious appetite!"

"You are a *bear*," the fox rebutted, as if that would end the argument.

"And you are a *fox*. You are cunning and devious. I am sure you are lying!"

And so they argued for hours, each blaming the other, until finally the fox said, "We will soon find out who has stolen the butter anyway."

"Is that so?" said the bear.

"Yes," the fox said confidently. He'd had a brilliant idea. "In the morning, whoever's tail is the greasiest must have been the thief who ate all that butter!"

The only question now was whether the fox would convince the bear that this was true…

"Hmm. Yes. What goes in must come out, I suppose," said the bear. "Now let's go home. I need to sleep again. I am far too upset. And the sooner we sleep, the sooner we will know who did it."

As the bear drifted into a deep sleep, the fox returned to the tree to collect the tiniest morsel of butter that was left behind. Before his stomach got the better of him, he scooped it on to his paw and ran back to the cabin. There, he found the bear sleeping on his stomach, as he usually did, and spread the remaining butter on to the bear's tail.

"There," he said to himself. "Problem solved!"

After a few hours, the bear awoke. "Good sleep?"

he asked while the fox pretended to rub the sleep out of his eyes.

"The best," he said with a mischievous smile. "Now shall we inspect our tails?"

They both left the cabin to inspect their reflections in the duck pond, looking over their shoulders at their respective tails.

"Oh my!" the bear gasped. "My tail... It's greasy!"

The fox looked down at his own tail, which he knew would not be greasy. "And mine ... is not!"

The bear was horrified at the sight. He was so certain it had been the fox who had eaten the butter. But his own tail...

"Fox," the bear said with a heavy heart, "I apologize. It appears it was I who ate the butter. I don't know when it happened, but..."

The fox waved away the bear's words before patting him on the shoulder. "Don't worry, my friend. It happens to the best of us."

"It does?" the bear asked, guilt written in the lines of his fur.

"It does," the fox answered. "Some of us are just better at getting away with it than others!"

SWEDISH FOLKTALES

It is a joy for me to share with you these Swedish tales of bravery and wishes that I remember from my childhood. They have always held a special place in my heart and have taught me the most important lessons. Even today, I carry them with me. I hope you'll enjoy the journey as you read about a selfless queen, a boy who will let nobody take his joy, and a magpie that teaches someone about the value of hard work.

LASSE, MY THRALL!

This is a story about wishes, taking things for granted and how the hand that feeds you can also take away. This tale was published in the 1883 book Sagor och Äfventyr Berättade på Svenska Landsmål. *You may notice it has similarities to the story of Aladdin and the lamp.*

Once upon a time, there lived a prince who spent his days travelling all over the world, spending his money on items he didn't need and people he didn't know, as if his wealth would never run out. But after his years of reckless spending, he found himself with almost nothing left and had no choice but to make his return home.

Late one evening on this journey, he spotted an old abandoned hut peeping out of the bushes. With his home more than two days away on foot and no money to lodge elsewhere, the prince decided that he would have to stay in the hut even though it was not fit for royalty.

When he entered the hut, he was surprised to find that there was nothing inside except for a great wooden chest against the wall furthest from the entrance. Curiosity overcame him. He opened the chest, but all he found inside was … another chest!

And within that, he discovered another chest.

And within that, another chest.

He opened all the chests until, finally, he pulled out a tiny box that held a slip of paper inside.

At first, the prince was wholly disappointed. All that effort for a slip of paper! But then he read out the intriguing words written on it. "Lasse, my thrall!" No sooner had he spoken those words than he heard a response.

"What would my master like?"

The prince looked around in surprise, but could not see where the voice had come from.

He repeated the words on the slip of paper in the hope of locating the voice. "Lasse, my thrall!"

Just as before, the voice asked, "What would my master like?"

The prince swivelled his head and peered around the room but found nobody. "If there is somebody here, please show yourself. And do get me something to eat as I am starving!"

The prince gasped in delight as, only a few moments later, a table appeared in front of him, laden with food and drink. He was so hungry he didn't even hesitate to inhale all that was in front of him.

When he was satisfied, nearly keeling over with exhaustion, he took up the slip of paper again.

"Lasse, my thrall!"

"What would my master like?"

"Now that I have been brought food, I require a bed in which to sleep. Though it must be an exquisite bed!"

His command was obeyed at once, and in front of him appeared a large, four-poster bed with a plump mattress fit for a king. As the prince lay down, he could not help but grin at how things had turned out. Who knew that this abandoned hut contained such treasures? Though the more he thought about it, the hut itself was far too wretched for all the fine things he was asking for.

"Lasse, my thrall!" he bellowed.

"What would my master like?"

"Well, as you can produce a feast and a bed fit for a king, surely you can produce a better room for me? You see, I am a prince after all, and I am accustomed to sleeping in better conditions!"

Nothing happened for some time, and so the prince thought his wishes had run out. Discontented, he rolled to face the wall and fell asleep.

But when he awoke in the morning, the room had been transformed. The wooden flooring was replaced with luxurious carpets, while the walls and ceilings were now covered with ornaments and decorations like those of a castle. And great arched windows allowed sunlight to stream into the room. When the prince stood up to look outside, he saw that even the raggedy bushes had now been replaced by a garden with roses of every variety. And when he explored further, he discovered the hut had grown to have more rooms than he could ever have imagined.

Despite all this, the prince was not happy. Although the hut now looked like the castle he called home, there was not a single other human in sight. There was not even a cat to keep him company.

He took up the scrap of paper once more and read, "Lasse, my thrall!"

"What would my master like?"

"Now that I have a suitable castle, I shall reside here. Though I cannot stay here by myself. I must have servants to care for me!"

And so maids and butlers appeared in his home, entering one by one, bowing and curtseying for their new master until the castle felt lively and homely, and the prince was finally content.

Meanwhile, on the opposite end of the forest from the prince's new castle, there so happened to be a king who lived in a castle of his own. The king had been there for many years and in fact owned the grounds of the forest itself and all that was built on his property. So when he looked out of his window, he could hardly believe what he saw: a rival castle!

"This is odd. I'm certain that was not there yesterday," the king said to himself before calling for his courtiers. "Tell me, do you see the castle across the forest, too?"

The courtiers' eyes widened with disbelief. "Why, yes, my king. It appears there is another castle."

The king's nostrils flared with fury. "Who dares to build a castle on my land!?"

The courtiers did not respond, afraid of their master's anger.

"Send for my soldiers and horsemen and tell them to tear down the castle immediately! Whoever is in that castle must go at once!"

The king's soldiers assembled in haste and set forth towards the prince's castle with great noise.

The prince heard them and quickly took up the scrap of paper. "Lasse, my thrall!" he yelled.

"What would my master like?"

"There are soldiers approaching, but I don't have any myself! Please provide me with twice as many soldiers and horsemen. Also pistols, muskets and a cannon! And be quick about it!"

It did not take more than a few minutes for soldiers with weapons in hand to line up outside the prince's castle. There were so many of them that the king's soldiers did not even dare advance! With his new men defending him, the prince marched up to the captain of the king's army.

"What is it you want?" he asked.

"The king wants you gone, for it is his land you reside upon," the captain explained.

"Well, I am not going anywhere! This is my land now. And you can see that I have many soldiers who will go to battle for me." The prince crossed his arms across his chest to assert his dominance. "But if the king chooses to have a conversation with me, perhaps we can be friends and come to an agreement. Perhaps I can even help him in battles against his enemies."

The captain considered the proposal and was pleased with the suggestion. So pleased in fact, that upon the prince's invitation, he together with his soldiers accepted something to eat and drink.

As they feasted inside the prince's castle, the captain let it slip that the king's daughter, who was an intelligent and beautiful woman, had yet not married.

"Why is that so?" the prince had asked.

"She can be very arrogant and hardly gives men the time of day. She supposes she has not yet met her match," the captain said in between bites. "Though I do think you could be suitable for her!"

"Perhaps I could be!" said the prince.

When at last the captain and his soldiers had left, the prince thought of the princess again and whether he should pay her a visit. She sounded interesting, certainly, and he was very curious.

"Lasse, my thrall!"

"What would my master like?"

"I would like to see the princess. However, I do not want to approach the king until I know a little more about her. As such, allow me to meet her in my dreams tonight!"

That night, as the prince slept, the princess appeared to him in a dream. She was just as beautiful and sharp-witted as the soldiers had told him, and they shared a conversation filled with warmth and laughter before the prince awoke.

That same morning, the king again looked out of his window and was surprised to see the castle across the forest still standing. He called for the captain and learned of the prince's offer to join forces. The king felt sick. He could not understand what powers or charms this prince had that he could cause his army of men to disobey orders. Then he became even more confused when his daughter came to tell him that she had awoken from a dream about the prince!

"I visited his castle. He was so handsome and wonderful and, oh, Father, I do want to marry him!" the princess said.

"But ... you have never even met him!" said the king in disbelief.

"I met him in my dreams, and that has taught me all I need to know," said the princess. "I want the prince to be my husband."

The king was furious about the prince's sorcery. First his captain and now his daughter! Just as he wondered what would be next, the king was informed that the prince had arrived, wearing his finest garments and accompanied by his advisers, assistants and other important persons, to seek the princess's hand.

The king put on his finest robe and crown before meeting the prince. Despite all the king's reservations, they were amicable and quickly became good friends as they discussed their affairs. The prince swiftly asked for the princess's hand in marriage and the king felt he could not refuse – the prince seemed kind and courteous after all, and it was better to have a powerful friend than a powerful enemy. However, the king insisted that he first must see the prince's castle. The prince agreed if the princess could also visit, to gauge whether his possessions be of her worth, and the king obliged.

When the prince returned home, he barked orders at Lasse to prepare for the princess's arrival, to which Lasse could only comply.

And when the king and princess arrived, they were so pleased that they decided there was no need to delay proceedings at all, and they rushed the wedding banquet to be held the very next day!

Once the wedding had taken place and celebrations were over, the prince returned to the castle with his new wife, both of them very happy to begin their new life together.

One evening, after some time had passed, the prince heard a familiar voice.

"Is master content now?"

Even though the prince could not see him, he knew it was Lasse. "Yes! Yes, I am! And if there is anything I can do for you, let me know," said the prince.

"I would very much like to have the scrap of paper you keep in the box," Lasse replied.

The prince laughed. How could he give something which had no flesh or blood a scrap of paper? Even so, he did as he was asked. "If that is all you want. I'm sure I have memorized the words by now anyway!"

Lasse thanked him and told the prince to lay the paper on the chair before he went to sleep and that he would fetch it then. And that is exactly what the prince did.

In the morning, when the prince awoke, to his horror the castle was freezing, and he saw that all that he once had was gone! He was no longer in a beautiful bed, his sleeping bride now instead sleeping on a mattress stuffed with straw. When he looked around, he noticed he was no longer in a castle at all but a small, rundown hut! With fear, he called out, "Lasse, my thrall!"

But no answer came.

"Lasse, my thrall!" he called again, and still there was no answer.

He soon realized what must have happened:

Lasse served the master who held the paper, and as Lasse now had the paper, he no longer had to serve the prince.

At the same moment, the king awoke in his castle and, as per usual, looked out of his window. But now he squinted in confusion. He could not see the castle where his daughter lived with the prince. He grew uneasy and called for his men to accompany him out through the forest to investigate.

There the king found his son-in-law with barely a shirt to his name and his daughter in tears.

"What on earth is going on?!" he demanded of the prince.

The prince did not respond, for he would rather die than admit how his own gullibility had led to him losing it all. The king could not understand what had happened but he knew he had been deeply deceived. He flew into a rage and ordered for the prince to be thrown in the dungeons immediately.

"No, you can't!" the princess pleaded to her father. "I love him!"

"But he has nothing. He cannot take care of you," the king responded. "Your tears are useless. He shall be locked away for ever!"

The king's men swiftly arrived to capture the

prince, restraining him with his hands tied behind his back as they marched him to the king's castle. As the prince was locked in a cell in the king's dungeon, he thought of how foolish he had been to give Lasse the scrap of paper. If only he hadn't!

"Oh, how silly you look!" a voice said.

When the prince looked up at where it came from, he saw a man had appeared through a small, barred window. In one hand, he waved a piece of paper. In the other, he held a basket of worn-out shoes. "Do you see all these shoes I have gone through, just trying to fulfil all of your wishes?"

It was Lasse! In a blink, the prince reached through the bars, snatched the scrap of paper from Lasse's hand and called, "Lasse, my thrall!"

And right away Lasse responded, "What would my master like?"

"Set me free from the dungeon at once and restore my castle and all my other wishes as they used to be. Including the princess!"

Lasse sighed but did as he was told. Within a few hours, all was returned to its place, and when the king awoke, he could see the castle from his window again. He wiped his eyes, but the castle remained! The king was perplexed and headed into the forest. There, he took off his crown to scratch his head, as he just did not understand how the castle was there when yesterday it had been gone. Even the gardens were as before!

"The devil must have a hand in this," he murmured to himself.

When the prince stepped out, he was even more shocked! "Did I not have you thrown in the dungeon only yesterday?"

The prince chuckled. "I think you must be confused! Why would you wish me ill? That is absurd! I am your daughter's husband after all!"

"But the castle … it was not here yesterday! And you hardly had any clothes to your name!"

The prince laughed at the king. "Oh, I do think your father is confused," he said to the princess, who had appeared behind him. "I wonder if the trolls of the forest have led you astray! Don't you think so, courtiers?"

The courtiers, who had come with the king, could not understand it either, but bowed in agreement and took the prince's side, for how else could it be explained?

The king looked around in shame. "I … suppose you must be right."

The prince was lucky. He had managed to fool the king and get his life back, but this time he did not take it for granted. No, now he did most things for himself rather than calling on Lasse for help.

The final task Lasse ever did for the prince was to put the scrap of paper in a little box buried seven feet underground, and to this day many are still digging and searching for it.

The prince was not one of them, for he had learned his lesson: one man's ease and luxury is another man's exhaustion and worn-out shoes. The same pair of hands that works for you can very easily turn on you if you treat them without care or gratitude.

JOLLY CALLE

This is the story of a boy who is joyful despite his circumstances and who sees beauty in everyday things without expecting anything in return. "Jolly Calle" was first translated into English by Danish-Swedish author Helena Nyblom.

Whoever said that money makes the world go round surely had never met a boy named Jolly Calle, aptly named because he was always jolly.

Although he was a poor boy and an orphan, he was always seen with a smile on his face. He would say, "I may not have any parents, but at one point I did, and if it were not for them then I would not have existed! And should I not be happy for existing at all?"

Even when it rained, Calle would laugh. "What's not to like about rain? Just listen to the soothing rhythm of the droplets! And they cool you down on a sweltering summer's day!"

And when stormy weather hit? Well, Calle was even happier! "Ah, the extreme winds only make my travels so much easier, I hardly have to use much force to push forward!" he would say. "I'm saving a fortune on rail fares!"

It seemed as if nothing, absolutely nothing, could bring Calle down.

One day, Calle was out in the woods when he saw an old brush lying near a tree trunk. He looked down at his shoes and noticed they were incredibly muddy. So he took the brush and used it to polish his shoes.

As he did so, Calle pondered his next steps. What could he do to ensure his livelihood? With his parents' death, Calle had never been taught any trade. He had made it this far, but he was due to run out of money and if he didn't earn more soon he knew he would starve.

It struck him – well, *two* things struck him – as he saw just how shiny his shoes had become: there are more pairs of shoes in the world than there are people, and those who wear shoes require them to be brushed.

Calle strolled along the road that led him to town with only the brush in his pocket and an idea. On his way, he stumbled upon a cornfield that he couldn't tear his eyes away from. He stopped by a narrow path, rows and rows of corn standing taller than himself, and sang to it.

"Just look at this delicious corn,
The gift that keeps us fed.
I take a bite and feel reborn,
For winter, have cornbread!"

Calle sang his song with fervour and excitement until a gruff voice interrupted him.

"Could you stop shouting? Besides, *you* were not the one who ploughed and sewed this corn!" The voice became angrier and soon enough Calle could see a farmer emerging from the field. "Neither you nor nobody else will reap this corn, nor will you grind it to make flour. It is mine and mine alone!"

Calle took off the red cap he was wearing. "I am sorry, sir. I did not mean to disrespect you."

The man merely huffed at Calle in response.

"But for what it's worth," Calle dared, "I do not believe I am entitled to the corn myself. I merely wanted to give thanks for this beautiful cornfield. I can now dance through it on my way to town, and to think I do not even have to pay you for the pleasure! And when you have reaped it all to feed yourself, and I hope others, it will only create more joy – and make my journey smoother, too – how wonderful!"

The farmer was mighty confused by Calle's positive attitude, but before he could question it, Calle was off again. He walked all day long until he reached the town. He stationed himself at a street corner with his brush, where he anticipated there to be much foot traffic, and waited to see if anybody would take him up on his business.

But, even after several hours, people simply passed him by, not so much as turning their heads to see what the orphan boy could offer them. Calle decided he would need to do more to make his presence known, and that his good nature might help him on his way.

Calle spat upon his brush and stood up just as a soldier passed by. Calle puffed out his chest and called out, "Do you need your shoes brushed, sir? I can be quick! I'm sure with just a little polish you will look even more commanding."

The soldier halted in surprise as he saw that the bold, friendly voice had come from this young boy. Despite being low on time, he allowed Calle to brush his shoes and was satisfied with just how shiny his boots now were.

A young woman passing by saw the satisfaction on the soldier's face, and Calle called out to her, "Would you like me to clean your shoes, miss? I can make them shine to match your eyes!" and the young woman came hurrying along gladly to have her shoes polished, too.

Throughout the day, a farmer, a solicitor, a maid and a scholar came along, and Calle had kind words for all of them. Soon enough, Calle's pockets were filled with coins from his customers. He decided he would allow himself a break.

Calle wandered through the town, admiring the buildings that towered above him and the fine mansions he could only dream of living in one day. But there was one building he couldn't look away from. It was adorned with pillars, statues and topiaries unlike any other, and there was a magnificent rose garden Calle swore he had smelled from the centre of town.

"Oh, what a beautiful sight! This house is a favourite of mine," Calle said to himself as he stood grasping its gilded spear-top railings.

"Of *yours*?" scoffed a footman who Calle had not noticed, for he had been standing as still as a statue at the entrance. "This mansion certainly is not yours. It belongs to Master Nabob – the richest man in town."

"Of course! I simply meant that this house is my favourite one to look at in town. Do tell Master Nabob that I am greatly obliged to him."

"Obliged? What do you mean?" the footman asked.

"Well, if it weren't for him, I would not get to appreciate such a sight! And so I am eternally grateful for his fortune."

"You are a weird one – anyone ever tell you that?" The footman shook his head. "The master did not build his mansion with you in mind, I must assure you. He has never heard of you. He built it to satisfy his own needs."

"That may be so," Calle said, beginning to walk away, "but all the same, he has made me happy, and surely my joy is worth more than he spent building the mansion!"

A day or two later, Calle ventured beyond town to seek more customers for his new business. After walking along the highway through light rain, he stopped at an inn, for he was thirsty and tired. He asked the innkeeper for a bowl of porridge, which he was granted, and he took a seat by the window overlooking the highway.

On the road not too far from him, Calle noted six wagons being drawn by oxen. He soon found out from the innkeeper that the wagons belonged to Master Nabob, who was sitting at a table over from him eating a rich stew out of a silver bowl. But Master Nabob did not look cheerful. In fact, even though his meal looked better than Calle's, his cheeks were sunken and his eyes dark as if he had just received the most disagreeable news.

"Well, that was absolutely scrumdiddlyumptious!" Calle announced as he shovelled the last of the porridge into his mouth.

"What was?" Master Nabob asked.

"Oh, this porridge!"

Master Nabob scrunched up his nose in disgust. "Would you rather not have a rich stew?"

"Gosh no! This porridge is just right for me," Calle exclaimed.

Once they had finished eating, they each tipped the boy who had served them. Master Nabob gave him a small coin while Calle gave a coin somewhat larger.

"Rich, are we?" Master Nabob asked Calle.

"Not at all. But after that porridge, I must pay him what he is due!"

The rich man simply shook his head at the boy.

After dinner, the rain had cleared and they both relocated to the garden of the inn. Master Nabob ordered for himself a variety of drinks and desserts, but none were to his liking. One drink was too strong, another too weak, and he did not even enjoy the pudding. His servants bent themselves over backwards, but nothing pleased him.

Meanwhile, Calle, seated a bit further away,

enjoyed himself with a glass of lemonade. He was so much enjoying the blue sky and the swaying of the trees above him that he could not help but laugh aloud.

"Is he laughing at me?" Master Nabob asked a servant boy.

"I will go and find out!" said the servant boy, and he raced over to Calle. "Are you laughing at Master Nabob?"

"Absolutely not," answered Calle. "I don't find him amusing at all."

The servant boy ran back to his master.

"Well?" Master Nabob asked.

"He is not laughing at you, sir. Though he did not say what he was laughing at."

Master Nabob furrowed his brows, irritated, but returned to his drinks. It did not take long before Calle began to laugh again, the fortunate weather enough to lift his spirits.

"What is he laughing at now?" Master Nabob asked the servant bitterly, and again the servant raced over to Calle to relay the question.

"Why, I am not laughing at anything!" Calle said – but this response did not appease his wealthy neighbour!

After a short while, Calle began to chuckle *again*, and this time he nearly fell over, bubbling with laughter.

"No, I do not understand. What is he laughing at? Me? The sky? What?" Master Nabob yelled at the servant. "You tell him that he can have all the coins he wants from me if only he will stop laughing!"

As the lad delivered Master Nabob's words, for once Calle became upset. He rarely ever got upset but even Calle had his limits. He tossed aside the coins he was offered and said, "If I cannot sit here and laugh, I will leave and enjoy myself elsewhere. It will cost me nothing to walk down the high road."

And so Calle left the inn garden and Master Nabob. Though he had only walked a short distance before Master Nabob caught up, riding along beside him in his gilded coach, followed by his six ox-drawn wagons.

"Would you like to drive with me?" the wealthy man asked Calle.

Calle smiled politely, but he was not interested. "I'd rather walk on such a beautiful day," he said.

At first, Master Nabob was taken aback by Calle's rejection. But after a moment's pause, he called for the coachman to stop, and stepped out. "May I accompany you, then, for a short way?"

"Why, of course," said Calle, taking Master Nabob's arm. Calle was so good-natured that he was quick to let go of his earlier frustration.

As they walked, Calle soaked in the warmth of the sun above him and focused his mind on the beauty of nature.

"I must say I have never met anybody like you," Master Nabob said. "I mean, I saw you through the curtains admiring my mansion, and you looked at it as if you were not the least bit envious. And at the inn, you did not envy my rich stew. You did not even envy the number of drinks I had at my seat in the garden."

"At your mansion, I was simply enjoying the sight of your beautiful home, and at the inn I was enjoying my own delightful porridge and lemonade. Why should I be envious?" said Calle. "You did not seem to be enjoying them yourself."

This took the rich man by surprise. "You know, you're right. Even with a grandiose house and garden, with many servants and horses, and anything I could wish to eat or drink, I feel empty. I am not happy. And you see, for the first time in my life, as I saw you simply enjoying yourself under the tree with your lemonade, I felt envious. I have never felt that before, for I have all that money can buy."

"Money does not buy everything, my good sir. You cannot buy sunshine or health or temper with money," said Calle.

"Oh yes, good temper! You have a *great* temper, and it makes you happy – so I must have it, cost what it may! Take all my wagons! All my coins!" Master Nabob took out a purse and began to open it.

Calle shook his head. "I cannot. But look, your fine shoes have become dusty from walking on the high road – allow me to clean them." Calle got out his brush and polished Master Nabob's shoes until they shone.

"What do I owe you?" asked Master Nabob.

"Nothing, sir. It was done in generous spirit."

"But … then … if you will not accept my money, what can I do? Why are you so happy, my dear boy?"

Calle broke out into the biggest smile. "Don't you see? I am happy for I am alive! Generosity, gratitude, happiness – they cannot be bought. You see, the poor have riches that the very wealthiest people cannot afford."

With that, Calle hopped over the stile and waved his red cap at Master Nabob. In a moment, he had disappeared into the meadow, leaving the master standing beside his ox-drawn wagons, his open purse still in his hand.

OLD HOPGIANT

In this tale, a giant assists a poor peasant in fighting for the land he is owed, and ultimately rescues him from his oppressor. It was first published in 1882 as "The Old Hop Giant" by August Bondeson.

Once upon a time, there were two neighbours, Ludvig, who was rich, and Oskar, who was poor, who, between them, owned a meadow. The idea was that the two would share the meadow equally, working to maintain it together, but Ludvig wanted it all for himself.

"If you do not agree to give up your half, I will drive you out of your home!" Ludvig shouted at Oskar.

"Well, I do not see a reason to give up my half just because you ask me to. Surely that is not fair!" cried Oskar.

"What would you like in *exchange* for your half then? Is that fair?"

"Indeed, it would be," Oskar agreed, "though there is nothing I want more than *keeping* my half of the meadow."

"Argh!" Ludvig grunted. "If you will not simply give it to me, I suppose we will have to play for it."

"What did you have in mind?" asked Oskar.

"Whoever mows the largest amount in a single day will become the owner of the entire meadow. That's fair, isn't it?"

Well, it sounded fair, but was it really? Ludvig had enough tools for the entire town while Oskar had barely anything to work with. However, he knew he had to either partake in the competition and put up a fight or simply agree to give away his half of the meadow.

"I will see you at dawn tomorrow," Ludvig said, taking Oskar's silence as agreement.

The two went inside their homes and gathered their equipment. Ludvig gathered as many mowers as he had, carefully cleaning off grass clippings and wiping away any grime that had gathered over the years. He even polished the mowers to give them an extra shine. Once all had been completed, he hired his strongest friends to come and help him mow the meadow the next day.

But Oskar wasn't faring so well. He only had one mower in his shed, which hardly functioned, and nobody to call to help him. He broke down in tears at the thought of how he was going to feed his cows without his half of the meadow. What would he do?

"What are you crying for?" a gruff voice asked. It was Oskar's other neighbour, who had popped his head over the fence that separated their two properties.

"I'm about to lose the meadow to *him* over there," Oskar responded, glaring in the direction where Ludvig lived.

"Why's that?"

When Oskar explained the competition that was due to take place tomorrow, the neighbour simply laughed at him.

"What's so funny?" Oskar asked.

"You're worrying for nothing. Look, what you ought to do is this: when the mowing begins, simply call out 'Old Hopgiant!' three times in succession."

"And that will help how?" asked Oskar.

"Oh, trust me, it will." The neighbour grinned before disappearing again, leaving Oskar with more questions than answers.

The next day, Ludvig had twenty of his friends ready to mow down one swathe of meadow after the other, while he simply watched from afar and barked orders.

"The meadow will be mine in no time," he had gloated to Oskar.

Oskar was sweating as he tried to mow strips of the meadow with his one lawnmower. He was about to give up when he remembered what his other neighbour had said last night. He had nothing else to lose, and so he yelled, "Old Hopgiant!"

Nothing happened and the mowers in the distance simply laughed at him.

He shouted again, ignoring the raucous laughter. "Old Hopgiant!"

Just as before, nothing happened, and the men in the distance were nearly falling over themselves laughing at Oskar's foolishness.

Then, for the third and final time, Oskar inhaled deeply before calling out with so much force it nearly shook his house, "*Old Hopgiant!*"

Oskar panted and wiped away the sweat that was dripping from his forehead. Then, when he looked up, he saw in the distance beyond the meadow a creature as tall as a ship's mast. He appeared like a cross between an ogre and a giant, and in his hand he carried a scythe larger than any tool Oskar had ever seen before.

He could hardly believe his eyes.

"Hey! What's that over there?" cried one of Ludvig's workers.

As the giant approached the meadow, he began wildly swinging and flinging his scythe, mowing the grass at a speed unknown to man. It only took a few minutes before half the meadow was mown!

Ludvig's men were crying out with fear, afraid of the strength that the creature displayed.

"Whatever that is, we stand no chance against it!" one man called out.

"I have a family at home! I can't afford to die!" another cried.

Within minutes, all of the men had dispersed, running as far away from the creature and the meadow as possible. Meanwhile, Ludvig flew into a rage.

"This is *my* meadow!" he bellowed as he rushed towards the giant creature. "And I will not allow anybody to take it from me!"

Ludvig ran forward boldly and, leaping as high as he could, gave the creature a good kick to no avail, as his foot got stuck to the giant's skin! When the giant looked down at where he had been struck, he was surprised to find a human and not a flea! In fact, he was so unbothered that he kept working away at the meadow, even with Ludvig's foot stuck to his leg. After all, he had a job to do!

Ludvig couldn't seem to tug himself free, and as the creature moved, he was forced to hop along after him, his other foot just reaching the ground, struggling to keep up.

"Ah, let me go!" he shouted at the giant. Unluckily for him, the giant was merrily hacking away at the grass, barely hearing anything except for the tune playing on repeat in his mind.

Then Ludvig thought to kick the giant with his *other* foot, hoping it would help set him free.

It didn't.

It, too, stuck to the giant, and now he hung from the back of the giant's leg, his arms dangling towards the ground and the blood rushing to his head while Old Hopgiant mowed the whole meadow.

"Will that be all, sir?" Old Hopgiant asked Oskar who stood in awe at the sight of the mowed meadow. "I think I hear my name being called again, so I must go immediately."

"Y-yes, that will be all. Thank you, my friend!" Oskar's eyes leaked tears of gratitude, for now the meadow was all *his,* and his cows would have a place to stay. No more bickering about how he should stick to his side of the meadow. No more sharing it with a neighbour who couldn't care less about the crops or the animals that depended on it. No more fears of losing it or being driven from his home.

"If you need me again, you know what to say!" Old Hopgiant winked at Oskar before marching away into the distance, disappearing into the fog.

And Ludvig? He had to go along with Old Hopgiant, hanging on to him like a rope!

THE QUEEN'S NECKLACE

In this story, a cruel king threatens his queen not to take off her pearl necklace. Despite the consequences, the brave, good-hearted queen is unfailingly kind and selfless. The original author of this tale is Helena Nyblom, one of Sweden's most revered fairy-tale writers.

Once upon a time, there was an old king who was wasn't very nice. In fact, some people would call him downright evil! He would berate his cooks for the slightest of mistakes and he would send his dogs to attack poor beggars who visited his doorstep looking for help. Simply put, the king did not care for people. He only cared for one thing: the necklace he had inherited from his mother.

It was a magnificent necklace strung with one hundred pearls. Ninety-nine of them were perfect – large and glowing – while the hundredth pearl was unlike the others in both size and shape. Even with its slight imperfection, the king thought the necklace his most prized possession, leaving it to rest in a jewellery box.

However, while the king had this great treasure and all the money a person could ask for, he had nobody to love. He had no family except for his nephew, Prince Nils.

One day, when Prince Nils came to visit his uncle, the king was in a terribly foul mood.

"What's wrong, Uncle?" Prince Nils asked.

"The king of Denmark just got married and he's rubbing it in my face – that's what's wrong!" barked the king.

"Should you not be happy for him?" said Prince Nils.

"No, for now he is better than me! He has something I haven't got: a wife." The king huffed. "Nils, I demand that you go to the countryside and find me a wife immediately. Yes, that is the only way I can be the most powerful again. She must be beautiful, of course. In fact, she must be *perfect*."

"Uncle, nobody is perfect," said Prince Nils. "Nothing can *ever* be perfect. Just look at your string of pearls!"

The king practically growled at his nephew, and the prince swallowed in fear. "I will try to find you a wife," he promised.

And so Nils rode through the countryside in search for a wife for his uncle. He met many women but none of them seemed like the right choice. One even laughed in his face. "Why would anyone want to marry the king? He is old and mean!" she scoffed.

The prince was on the verge of giving up when he rode past a farm deep in the countryside, where a young woman was laughing at something over a fence.

"Look at these little chickens! Aren't they just the most beautiful chicks you have ever seen? And these flowers! Look at how they sway in the wind!" She shook her head in awe. "Isn't everything just so delightful you must laugh?"

Nils was struck by the warmth the woman radiated.

"What is your name?" he asked her.

"Blanzeflor," the woman replied. "It means 'white flower'."

"Blanzeflor, could I speak to your father, please? I have been sent by the king," said Prince Nils.

Blanzeflor led Nils to her father, who was cleaning the stalls of the stable.

"How can I help you?" he asked.

"I am here to ask if you will allow your daughter to marry the king," said Prince Nils.

"The king wants to marry *my* daughter?" the farmer gasped. Blanzeflor, too, looked incredibly surprised.

Nils nodded. "Indeed. I believe your daughter would be perfect for him."

The father looked to his daughter. "It is your choice, Blanzeflor. This is a huge opportunity, though I have heard rumours about the king... Not good ones."

"I know. I have heard them, too," admitted

Blanzeflor, "but I am certain I can soften the king."

Nils looked at Blanzeflor sorrowfully, guilt creeping in. She had high expectations of what she could do, but she had not met his uncle yet and the stories she had heard were most likely only a fraction of the truth. Even the stories about the king could not do his cruelty justice. But Nils knew what he had been tasked to do, and he hoped Blanzeflor was right.

When Nils and Blanzeflor arrived back at the castle, the king was overjoyed.

"My, she is perfect!" he gloated. "Now let us get married!"

The wedding was grand and majestic, held in the royal church in front of thousands of people. Nils stood by as the bishop declared the king and Blanzeflor man and wife. Again, the guilt about his part in their marriage reared its head. He tried to commit the sound of Blanzeflor's laugh to his memory as he worried that the king would soon make it disappear for ever.

Nils's guilt grew as he watched the king fasten his most precious possession, the string of pearls, around his new wife's neck.

"You must always wear them," the king commanded. "You must never disobey me…" The threat was as clear as day: if Blanzeflor took off the necklace, she would also lose her head.

And so began Blanzeflor's new life as a queen. Over time, Blanzeflor's easy smile and laughter began to fade, as the king wore her down with his cruelty. The only joys that kept Blanzeflor going were the kindness of Prince Nils and the birds outside her window. Every day, she would open it and look out at the spectacular view of the sky and the birds that flew through it. In the winter, she would scatter crumbs on her windowsill, nursing the hungry birds through the cold.

One night, Blanzeflor heard a noise just before she fell asleep. Sitting up, she saw a small stone with a note tied to it had been thrown through her window and landed on the carpet. Quickly she lit a candle and read the note.

Queen Blanzeflor takes pity on the birds,
but does she pity people of her town?
I am a poor widow with no home, nine
children and only one coat.
Please, help us!

When Blanzeflor looked out of the window, she saw nobody there. The queen shed tears over the note and the person who had written it. Subconsciously, her fingers moved to her necklace, and a plan began to form in her mind.

The next morning, she called Nils to her side and gave to him a single pearl from the necklace.

"What are you doing?" he asked her.

"I received a note from a poor woman with nine children and only one coat. Take this to the village and give it to her. She needs it more than I do."

Nils was perplexed at the request, but obeyed the queen nonetheless. He took the pearl and rode to the village, where a woman stood with nine children surrounding her, all trembling from the cold as their mother tried to cover them all with only one coat.

"A gift," he said to the widow, handing over the pearl, "from Queen Blanzeflor."

The woman wept with gratitude. "A pearl from the pearl of our kingdom!"

That same evening, the queen came down for dinner with her husband and, as predicted, nobody noticed a pearl missing from around her neck. She breathed a sigh of relief.

But that evening another stone with a note tied

around it came through her window. This time it was from a fisherman.

The king claims that the eels in the river
belong to his estate and that we cannot catch them.
But if that is the case, how are we to make a living?
How are we to live at all? Tell us, my queen,
how are we to go on? Not just us fishermen,
but the hungry townsfolk themselves?

Again the queen wept, and again she gave Nils another pearl to give away. When the fisherman received the queen's gift, he cried with appreciation.

"How could such a heartless king have married such a kind woman?" he asked as Nils walked away.

Every night after that, a stone was thrown into the queen's room by another person asking for her help. And every day, the queen pulled another pearl from her necklace and sent for Nils to give it away to someone in need.

"My queen, nearly half the pearls have been given away. The king will notice their absence soon," Nils warned her, worried.

Blanzeflor laughed. "No, he won't. Just look!" She pulled the pin from her long braid and let her hair fall down her back, hiding the part of the necklace with missing pearls. "My hair will cover their absence. There is nothing to worry about, Nils."

But with every day that passed, the pearls around Blanzeflor's neck decreased, and soon her hair wasn't enough to conceal the missing pearls! Even so, the selfish king did not notice – and her generosity did not stop either.

Blanzeflor was so generous that Nils couldn't help but become enchanted by her generosity. In a moment of awe, when she asked him to remove a pearl for the less fortunate, he snuck the imperfect pearl to keep for himself.

For ninety-nine days, Blanzeflor gave pearl after pearl from her necklace to the less fortunate. At last there was not a single pearl left around her neck.'

When the king saw Blanzeflor enter the banquet hall with a bare throat, he flew into a fit of rage. "Where is my string of pearls?" he demanded.

The queen attempted to appear relaxed, pretending she had forgotten all about the king's warning about never taking off the necklace. "I took it off as it needs a polish. Wearing it every day isn't good for the pearls, my dear."

The king turned to the maid, distrusting his

wife's story. "Find Blanzeflor's pearls and deliver them to me immediately!"

The maid went looking for the necklace in the bedchamber but came up empty-handed. When she returned, she hung her head in shame. "I am sorry, Your Majesty, but I could not find them."

The king was furious. He leaned over Blanzeflor, his face as red as a tomato, and thundered, "What have you done with my pearls?"

Blanzeflor said nothing to the king. She refused to betray those she had helped. She knew in her heart that she had done nothing wrong, even if the king would never see it that way.

"Find my pearls!" he bellowed to the room. "Immediately!"

His lords and ladies scurried around the castle, trying to locate the necklace, but even as they tore through all the rooms, they found nothing...

Until one person looked under a pillow and found the imperfect pearl.

"Where did you find this?" the king demanded.

"Under Prince Nils's pillow, Your Majesty."

The king ordered for his men to drag Nils to him. "How could you steal from me, Nils?" he bellowed at his nephew.

Nils said nothing. How could he explain? He had kept the pearl as a token of his love for Blanzeflor, which had grown over time, sparked by her kindness to others.

"You will lose your head, dear nephew. At dawn! And so will she." The king pointed at his wife. "If she hadn't taken off that necklace, my nephew would not have been tempted to steal. This is all her fault."

Nils and Blanzeflor were sent to cells in the dungeon below the banqueting hall. Their cells had a communicating window so they could speak with each other.

"I'm so sorry, Nils," Blanzeflor said through sobs.

"No, don't be. If I hadn't kept that last pearl, maybe we wouldn't be here," Nils said with a heavy sigh.

The next morning, Nils woke to find a flock of birds at the window of his cell. They softly sneaked between the bars and gathered around him in the dungeon. To his surprise, they spoke to him.

"Without fail, she fed us," tweeted the blackbird.

"She cared for me when my wing was injured," trilled the blue tit.

"We must save her. We *will* save her," chirped the sparrow.

When Blanzeflor awoke, she saw birds gathered on the windowsill. She smiled at them, remembering how they used to greet her each morning in her bedchamber.

"You've found me! Though I must apologize. I have nothing to give you," she sighed.

But the birds did not care that she had nothing to give. Instead, they flew through the bars of the window and joined her in the dungeon. They circled her, before one by one they dropped what appeared to be shimmering pearls into her lap.

"This is the tear you shed over the widow with the nine children," sang the waxwing.

"This tear was wept for the fisherman," rasped the magpie.

More and more birds flocked around her, dropping tears that transformed until her lap was filled with enchanted pearls that brightened the dark cell.

"Thank you, thank you!" she cried, laughing for the first time in many long months.

But her laughter did not last long, for the king and his armed men soon entered. One man was especially frightening, as he wore a black hood and carried a sharp axe. Blanzeflor knew he was the man sent for her head.

The king stepped inside the dungeon where his wife sat. "What a shame it had to end this way, but treachery cannot go unpunished." He gave a dark chuckle – but then he froze, seeing the heap of pearls in her lap. How could it be that they were in front of her now? Had she had them all along and simply been hiding them from him? *Where* had she been hiding them? "My pearls! No, they cannot be…"

He attempted to call for his men, when, suddenly, he clasped his hand to his chest. The king collapsed to the floor with a thud. Blanzeflor fell to her knees beside him, the pearls in her lap scattering around her as she wept for her husband, so shocked to see his stolen pearls that his heart had stopped.

The men who stood outside the dungeon bowed before her while the executioner tore off his hood and threw his axe aside. "You are free, my queen. As are you, Nils. Our new sovereign, King Nils!"

It did not take long before news of the wicked king's death had reached the neighbouring villages. Many rejoiced, and soon there were festivals taking place to celebrate the coronation of the new king.

One day, Blanzeflor asked Nils, "Why did you keep the pearl?"

Nils's cheeks reddened. "It was a token of my love for you, my queen."

The queen smiled. She, too, had grown very fond of Nils, and it was only a matter of days before they got married.

At the wedding, it was as if the entire village had changed. People laughed again and danced in the street without a care. Birds were rollicking in the sky. Even those less fortunate came to celebrate the new union, hopeful for the future.

The only person who was disappointed was the executioner, who had returned to the dungeon in the hope of collecting all the pearls that had fallen from Blanzeflor's lap. He was planning to sell each and every one of them for a mighty penny.

But when he searched the dungeon, he only found pools of water The pearls the birds had dropped in the queen's lap had turned themselves back into tears.

THE MAGPIE WITH SALT ON HIS TAIL

It is believed that the legend of salting a bird's tail began in the sixteenth century, though it may even have been earlier than that. Traditionally, sprinkling salt on the tail of a magpie – which in Scandinavia has been thought to be a witch in disguise – renders the bird temporarily incapable of flying, makes it easy to capture and may even grant a wish or two!

Making a wish isn't hard at all. In fact, it's the easiest thing to do in the world. But to make that wish a reality? Well, that is something else entirely. And nobody learned that lesson better than our lazy boy, Olle, who wanted and wanted but would do nothing to make his wishes come true. He wished for things so often that his mother teased him about it.

"And what are we asking for today, Olle?" she would ask every morning before she headed out to work.

"A pocketknife! Or perhaps a sled! Or..." And so instead of helping his mother with any of the household chores, Olle spent his time wandering, daydreaming and listing all the things he wanted.

Olle and his mother had been poor ever since Olle's father passed away many years ago, so they could afford little. Every minute of every day, he would think of something new to wish for.

One day, as he was out and about, he spotted an old man sitting on a bench with his eyes closed.

"Are you OK, old man?" Olle asked.

"Oh yes, I'm just ... resting," the man replied.

Olle was relieved. The man was so still Olle had worried he may have been dead!

"Would you like some advice?" the old man asked the boy, his eyes now wide open with a sparkle in them.

Olle frowned. He didn't exactly *want* unsolicited advice, but he figured that it couldn't hurt. "Go on then, old man."

The old man broke into a smile. "I hear you wandering these streets, wishing and wishing, but how often do they come true?"

"They don't," Olle admitted.

"Exactly. But I know how you can change that."

"Is that so?" Olle asked, his hopes rising.

The old man nodded. "Have you heard of the legend of the magpie?"

Olle shook his head.

"They say that if you sprinkle a pinch of salt on the tail of a magpie, anything you wish for will come true. Go to the woods and find one. There is only one catch..."

"What?" Olle held his breath in anticipation.

"You must make your wish quickly! If the salt falls off the magpie's tail before you've made your wish, it won't come true."

"But if it doesn't, I'll get anything I ask for?"

"Indeed, my son."

Olle could hardly contain his excitement. Within minutes, he had run home to retrieve a bag of salt large enough to grant him a hundred wishes and shoved it deep into his pocket. Without stopping for breath, he ran into the forest in search of a magpie.

Olle thought it would be easy to sprinkle salt on the tail of a magpie, but boy was he wrong! What the old man *didn't* tell Olle was that magpies cannot be as easily fooled as say a pheasant or a duck. No, magpies are intelligent birds – if not one of the most intelligent animals to exist.

So even though Olle saw many magpies in the forest, he was disappointed to find that the black-and-white birds with the shiny blue-green wings flew away before he could get close to them. In fact, sometimes they seemed to taunt him, waiting for him to get very close until they flapped away, their caws like laughter. Olle sat down, exhausted, between the trees, the hope he once had dissipating.

"My wishes will never come true," he sighed to himself as he leaned against the rough but comforting trunk of a pine tree. Olle was just drifting off to sleep when he heard something…

"Olle! Olle!" a voice called.

Olle looked up and, in between the branches, he could see it: a magpie looking down at him.

"You can talk?" he exclaimed.

"Yes!" the magpie answered. "I hear that you want your wishes to come true. Is that right?"

"Yes, it is!"

"Well, I can help you. But you will need to help me first..."

Olle sat up straight, his neck straining from looking up at the magpie. "What do you need?"

"I need a knife – a *fine* knife – to clean my claws. If you bring one to me, I will sit still long enough for you to sprinkle salt on my tail!"

A knife for a wish. It was simple enough, right? Surely the magpie wouldn't lie to him. Yes, the other magpies had teased him, but this one spoke! He seemed honourable enough.

"OK, I will get you a knife," Olle promised.

But of course Olle had no money. How could he ever afford a fine knife? All the knives at home were dull with use. Olle thought for a moment until he realized he knew exactly what to do. In the forest there were enough berries to feed an entire village. Olle decided he could use this to his advantage.

The next day, Olle returned to the forest with one bucket in each hand and filled them up with berries he picked from the bushes. Blueberries, cloudberries, lingonberries and blackcurrants stained his fingers, but it was worth it. When he took them to the market, the townsfolk couldn't help but be charmed by the labour of his hands and buy all of his goods.

By the end of the day, Olle could afford to buy a cheap pocketknife. It wasn't a *fine* knife, but he was sure it was sharp enough to do the job.

Before returning to the forest the next morning, he filled his pocket with salt. Olle was about to get his wish!

"Oh, magpie! I've got your knife!" he called out as he arrived at the same pine tree he visited only the day before yesterday.

The magpie flew down to where Olle stood and took one look at the knife before shaking his head and flapping his wings with agitation. "That will not do! Have you seen the material? I require the finest steel. Not whatever copper this is!"

Before Olle could make a case for how hard he had worked for the knife, the magpie had flown up into the tree.

"OK, what if I get you a *better* knife?" he yelled. "Will that do?"

"No, it will not. Now what I really want is a sled."

"A *sled*?" Olle queried. What could a magpie do with a sled?

"Yes, a sled. I'm quite tired of using my wings, you know."

Olle could not imagine the magpie on a sled, but if it would get him his wish…

"I will get you a sled!" Olle promised.

And so, with the pocketknife the magpie had rejected now in his possession, Olle began thinking of other ways to make money. He could only get so far by picking and selling berries, so Olle thought of something more lucrative he could do. He could use the knife to whittle spoons, bowls and wooden toys to sell at the market! Satisfied with his new idea, he set to work.

Again, the townspeople could see the time and effort that Olle had put into crafting his items, and it only took a few days before he sold out and was able to buy a used sled.

Once again he went to the forest, his pockets lined with salt, and presented the sled to the magpie.

"What is this you have brought me? This is not what I wanted!" the magpie screeched before flying off into one of the branches.

Olle sighed. "It's a sled! Wh—"

"No, what I really want now is a wagon!"

Olle couldn't believe the magpie's ingratitude, but what choice did he have? Soon he was on his way once more. He began whittling again, but this time he used his new sled to make deliveries outside of town to reach folks with deeper pockets. He was soon able to keep some money aside to help out his mother with their household costs.

Once he had made enough money to afford a wagon – not a used one but a *new* one – he returned to the forest.

The magpie strutted across the wagon with its beak turned up. "This is not the one I want!"

Olle was so disappointed. He couldn't please the magpie, it seemed, no matter what he tried. "OK, I will get ano—"

"No, actually," the magpie said, "what I *really* want is a fine horse and carriage."

"Sorry?"

"Yes, a horse and carriage!"

Olle couldn't imagine what the magpie would

do with the horse and carriage, but again he went away to earn some more money.

He continued whittling and making deliveries, but now that he had a wagon, he was also able to haul firewood across the country for people to burn in the winter. Working hard at both trades, Olle was able to support his mother and eventually earn enough to afford a horse and carriage fit for royals.

But when the magpie saw the horse and carriage, he was not impressed. "I do not particularly like the colour of this horse!" he complained.

Olle shook his head. Why could he not get it right?

"OK, I will get you—"

"A house? Yes, that is what you will get me. It is getting mighty cold out here and I do need to stay warm. Unless you don't want your wish, that is?"

So Olle went back to work, carving and delivering. However, he soon found it too much for one person, so he hired other boys to help him with the trade. His business had soon expanded so much that he was able to move out of his mother's house and buy a nice little home at the edge of town, near the forest where the magpie resided. From his yard, he called for the magpie and presented the house.

"What is this? This is not a house! This is a shed for peasants! I require a castle!"

Olle was hurt by the magpie. He had spent time, money and energy on this house. How could the magpie not see that?

"OK, fine, I will buy you a castle, but then—"

"No, a castle won't do. What I need now is an abundance of gold coins. Then I can buy all that *I* want without having to go through *you*."

Olle thought that, for once, the magpie might be right. So much could have been avoided if only the magpie had chosen the things he desired himself. So Olle worked even harder. He saved carefully and expanded his business, eventually earning enough money to buy not just one castle but two.

When he showed the magpie a sack overflowing with gold coins, the magpie finally said, "*That* is what I wanted. You have done well, Olle. Now you may sprinkle the salt on my tail and make your wish once and for all."

Olle broke into a huge smile. The time had come! At long last! He retrieved the salt from his pocket and sprinkled it on to the magpie's tail.

"What is your wish, Olle?" the magpie asked.

Olle thought about it. What did he wish for?

All this time, he had been so busy working and earning money that he had completely forgotten what it was he wished for! When he had first set out to have his wish granted by the magpie, he had been poor and could afford very little. But now he could not think of a single thing that he wanted.

The magpie gave Olle three seconds, but Olle could not come up with anything. The magpie flipped his tail with a laugh, and off flew all the salt Olle had sprinkled on it.

Olle was filled with anger and frustration, feeling tricked by the magpie. Finally, he thought of what he wanted and announced, "I want a cage that I can put you in!"

"Now that's not very nice," the magpie said with a frown. "Why would you want to do that? Have I not given you all that you wanted?"

"You have not given me anything!" Olle exclaimed.

"No?" The magpie titled his head quizzically. "Because of me, did you not end up with a knife? And a sled and a wagon and a..." The magpie reeled off all the things he had requested from Olle and turned away, and Olle realized these were things that *he himself* had wanted.

"And did you not get all of this without a single wish?" said the magpie. "Don't you see? You got all of this with hard work. Don't you think this lesson was a greater gift than any wish?"

Stunned, Olle realized the magpie was right. He had attained all those things he once could only dream of without making a single wish. He had earned them *himself*.

"You're … you're right," Olle conceded.

But the magpie had flown off, a single speck of salt still sticking to his tail.

ABOUT THE AUTHOR

Anika Hussain was born and raised in Stockholm, Sweden, but now lives and writes in Bristol. She has made TV and radio appearances in Sweden, speaking about the impact writing has had on her life, the importance of representation, and her work with The Ministry of Storytelling. Anika is also a graduate of the Bath Spa MA Writing for Young People. When not writing, you can find Anika yelling at the TV about inconsistencies or listening to true-crime podcasts. She also loves corgis with a scary passion.